Frank Trollope

The Gladstones

A Novel: Vol. II.

Frank Trollope

The Gladstones
A Novel: Vol. II.

ISBN/EAN: 9783337043858

Printed in Europe, USA, Canada, Australia, Japan

Cover: Foto ©Andreas Hilbeck / pixelio.de

More available books at **www.hansebooks.com**

THE GLADSTONES.

A NOVEL.

IN THREE VOLUMES.

BY

FRANK TROLLOPE,

AUTHOR OF

"THE MARKED MAN," "BROKEN FETTERS," "AN OLD MAN'S SECRET,"
"A RIGHT-MINDED WOMAN," &C.

VOL. II.

LONDON:

T. CAUTLEY NEWBY, PUBLISHER,
30, WELBECK STREET, CAVENDISH SQUARE.
1872.

CHAPTER I.

SARAH CRISP did not go home immediately after leaving Frances Gladstone; she took her way through some bye lanes to the upper end of Braidsworth, and after a rapid walk of a quarter of an hour, found herself standing opposite a humble cottage with a garden in front, apparently well stocked with vegetables and common flowers. It was the home of Mrs. Jobson, the mother of the young man who was Sarah's lover.

Sarah could see, through the blind of the lower window, that Mrs. Jobson was comfortably seated in a large arm-chair, either asleep or in a meditative mood, for there was no appearance of work on the table near which she was sitting. When the door opened Mrs. Jobson made no movement, for she supposed it was her son Harry come home to supper, and without looking round, said—

"Come, lad, thou'st been ever sin' eight o'clock, and it's time thou hadst thy supper."

"It's not Harry, Mrs. Jobson," said Sarah, in a timid voice.

"Bless us! Sarah Crisp, what a fright thou's given me," cried the honest creature, starting up. "Come this way, my bairn, and sit thee down abit. Harry's away at the fire at Mr. Gladstone's foundry, and I'm quite weary o' waiting for him."

"I've just come from it," said Sarah, placing a chair near Mrs. Jobson, "there's a large number of people there."

"Far more than'll be of any use, I warrant," said the old woman, reseating herself; "and how's thy mother and the poor little bairn?"

"Mother's sadly, and Jessie no better," said Sarah, trying to speak calmly.

"Harry's awful 'feared thou'lt tak' the fever, my lass," said Mrs. Jobson, with a candour that brought the blushes into her companion's cheeks; "it's his first thought in the morning and his last o' neets, Sarah."

"Harry is too good," said the girl, with a faint smile. "I've not seen him these two or three nights."

"Then what comes of him, Sarah?" demanded the mother, anxiously, "he's drank his tea like one demented every neet o' coming home, and been off again as if he'd every body's work to do as well as his own. I thowt he'd be ganging to thee, lass."

"I've not set eyes on him since Saturday," rejoined the girl; and, anxious to change the subject, she continued her talk about the fire. "I'm afraid 'twill ruin Mr. Gladstone, and many more into the bargain."

"I'm sorry for him, lass, because he's been a good master, and—"

"And a kind one, as well," interrupted Sarah.

"Yes, and a kind one," rejoined Mrs. Jobson, "and there's but few of the sort now-a-days. Harry often says what a pity it is he doesn't join the Union."

"Father doesn't like the Union any more than Mr. Gladstone does," continued Sarah, remembering many bitter words William Crisp had launched forth, in anger, at this combination of workmen against their masters. "Do you know, mother, what it is they want?"

"'Deed no, my lass; an auld woman like me cannot fash to understand all the notions these younkers get into their silly pates, now-a-days; and Harry's gone clean daft wi' their Union schemes—more's the pity. I wish thou'd put him off it a bit."

At that moment Harry rushed in, heated and flushed, as if he had been running, and on seeing Sarah he went up to her and gave her a hearty shake of the hand.

"Where hast been till this time o' neet,

lad ?" demanded his mother, who began bustling about to get the supper placed on the table. " Sarah has been wi' me half-an-hour or more."

"I'm sorry I didn't know, mother," was the rejoinder, " I've been down at the fire."

" Helping to put it out, I'll be bound," said Mrs. Jobson, complacently. " Harry, Harry, thoul't be doing thyself a mischief one of these odd days."

Sarah saw in a moment that he had not, for his hands and clothes were too clean for that. She was making her comments on this, in her own mind, whilst Mrs. Jobson went on with her preparation for supper, and Harry began to give them an account of what he had seen.

" Thou can tell us the rest after supper, lad," said his mother, when she had put the crusty loaf and cheese and mugs of beer on the table. " Draw up thy chair, Sarah, and let Harry ask a blessing."

Sarah, however, would not stay, as she feared her father might return before she got home, and want his supper, on this night above all others, and, as they both knew, her mother had Jessie to attend to.

"Only take a bit and a sup, at any rate," urged Harry, putting his arm familiarly round her waist to detain her.

"I really cannot, Harry, dear," she said, turning to him with tears in her eyes. "You, of all folks, shouldn't hinder my going."

"Then I'll go home with thee, Sarah," he said, taking up his hat. "Mother, I'll be back in a few minutes."

"Harry! Harry! it's close upon twelve o'clock!" cried his mother, in a shrill voice. "If Sarah Crisp will go, let her go by herself."

"I can run home in five minutes, Harry, dear," whispered Sarah, who was growing more and more nervous, as her lover seemed to persist in his wish. "Stay with your mother, and let me go alone."

"Bid the old woman good night, and come

away," said he, in a determined tone, as he strode to the door, and Sarah, seeing there was no help for it, bade Mrs. Jobson goodnight, and followed him out.

Harry was very nigh calling himself a fool for his pains, when he found how silent and queer his companion behaved during the walk home, short as it was; and when they parted at her father's door the hand he held in his own scarcely returned the hearty pressure by which he attempted to express his affection for her.

The house was in total darkness, and it was with some difficulty Sarah managed to grope her way to the stairs intending to go to her mother's room, where she knew a light could be obtained.

She went up so quietly that Mrs. Crisp apparently did not hear her, for she did not alter her position when Sarah opened the door and stepped into the little room. One glance at the bed showed that all was over, and that Jessie's pure and peaceful spirit had deserted

its earthly tabernacle. The mother had laid
the dead body of her child upon the bed, and
was now sitting rocking herself in her chair,
accompanying the action with a low, moaning
sound, that was tenfold more appalling than
would have been the most violent outburst of
grief.

Sarah took off her shawl and bonnet, and
creeping up to the bedside, kissed the wasted
brow and lips, closed Jessie's eyes, and folded
the little arms over the breast. She had not
long passed away, for the wan cheeks had not
that clammy feeling that makes the blood run
cold when we touch those who have been some
time dead. There was so little appearance of
death about the child, that had not Sarah
known the unerring signs, she could almost
have fancied the poor little thing was in a
peaceful sleep.

"Mother, dear, you had better go down
stairs a bit," she said, when she had accomplished the last sad offices of love.

"Oh, Sarah! why did you and your father

go out, and leave me alone to see the last of my child ?" sobbed the afflicted, heart-broken parent. " She cried out sorely for you both at the last, the sweet lamb! and for Tommy and Bobby, too, and a hard parting she had."

Sarah was too much pained by her mother's upbraiding to defend herself, or she would have said that neither her father nor herself would have left the house had they known how ill Jessie really was. She went and laid her head on her mother's lap, as she had done many a time when she had committed any childish fault, and Mary Crisp wept over her, and forgave her, and then they both turned to the bed, and permitted their sorrow to spend itself over all that remained of the object of their devoted love.

They had become calm and composed again by the time William Crisp returned, wet and weary with his three hours' exhausting toil. He knew at once by the averted looks with which his wife and daughter received him, of the solemn change that had passed over his household since he had left it, and with a deep " God's will be done, Mary !" he, too, advanced to the head of the bed, and kissed the cold cheek of his child.

The father's grief did not spend itself in loud and unavailing sorrow, for his feelings were too deep and stern for that. One passionate kiss imprinted on the senseless brow was all that told them how tender and fond had been his love ; but the stillness that came over his spirit thereat was much more awful than any violent outburst of grief could have possibly been.

When his wife spoke to him in the tender accents of their early days, he did not answer her, but sat absorbed and silent as if his spirit was entirely crushed by the weight of sorrow it had to bear.

" Go down stairs, Sarah, and get thy father some supper," said Mrs. Crisp, in calm, sad tones, and then, as her daughter obeyed the bidding, the wife went up to her husband and said—

" Our sainted bairn's last words, William, were to send her love to thee. ' Kiss daddy for me,' she said, and died upon my breast."

" And I was not here to see it," groaned the father.

" Thou wast where God was pleased to call thee, William," said his wife, taking his hand. " Mr. Gladstone has been a good friend to you and yours, and it would have been a wicked thing in thee to have held back thy hand from helping him in his need."

Mary had never before endeavoured to teach her husband his duty to his fellow men ; but now, inspired by the sight of his strong unspoken grief, she ventured upon a course which at another time she would not have dared to follow.

" Thank God, she has been taken from the evil to come !" groaned the desponding father. " Oh, wife ! there are dark days in store for all of us !"

" We must bear them patiently, William,"

she said, with sublime despair. "Are we not yet spared to each other?"

He caught her in his arms, and kissed her wasted cheek, with the same passionate fondness that he had just lavished upon his dead child, and then his grief found vent, and the devoted pair wept and prayed by turns.

"Our child is happy now," sobbed the mother, as she sat with her head resting on her husband's breast. "The summer's heat and the winter's cold will never try her poor crippled limbs again; very fondly she loved the first daisies and primroses that Bobby and Tommy could bring her from Braidsworth Wood, and the robin's eggs Harry Jobson found for her."

And going to a closet she brought out a few withered flowers and a string of birds' eggs, which Jessie had placed there the very night before she was taken ill of the fever.

Poor mother! they will be more precious to you than all the money that a monarch could bestow.

Three days after, one of those simple family funeral processions, which make one ten times more sad with its plain unmistakeable air of struggling poverty than all the rich trappings of horses, feathered hearse, and numerous mourning coaches, with which wealth invests the last sad rites of humanity, might be seen winding up Braidsworth Lane towards the churchyard; the small coffin came first, on which was marked Jessie's name and age, and after it came William Crisp supporting his wife, whose feeble steps showed how painful was the effort she made to see her child put decently into the grave. Crisp looked dark and stern, and there were some that wondered how he could show so little emotion. Whilst others asserted death had already set its seal upon his ashy brow, and that he would go long before the poor, delicate wife he half carried with him.

A stout, florid countenanced man followed with Sarah, who looked exceedingly thin and pale beside him, and many of the spectators said there must be something wonderful in country air and country living to account for the difference between Mary Crisp and the man who was her brother; they did not reflect that disease, care, and grief rob the cheek of its bloom far more surely than the close confinement of a town.

Thus the solemn procession went through the green lane, the air sweet with the scent of hay, and musical with the glad melody of summer. It was one of those bright days that the dead child had loved so well when in life, with a soft breeze whispering around the flowers, and the wild bees humming blithely on the wing. There was nothing mournful or sad around save in the hearts of those who went up to the old churchyard, where the sunlight lay soft upon the graves. May it shine as fair upon the Resurrection.

CHAPTER II.

"Gladstone's foundry made a capital blaze, Mr. Philips, as one would wish to see," said a harsh voice close to the elbow of the senior partner of the firm of Philips and Young, as he jogged home on his black mare soon after midnight, after all fear of the fire spreading had ceased. " It was a devilish fine sight, in my opinion, and many more than me were pleased to see it. It will teach you and your blood-sucking brother manufacturers a tidy lesson. We poor working men will get our rights, I should think, now."

"I have not the pleasure of knowing you, I think," stammered the timid Mr. Philips, edging his horse as far away from the speaker as he could. "What is your name?"

"It might not be quite convenient to tell you," said the other, with a sneering laugh. "Suppose you call me Ned Browne as long as our roads are together. It's a good three miles yet to your place, and I've got to go further than that, and am not fond of travelling by myself such a lonely road," laughing at the evident fright of his companion.

"I wish I was safely at home," thought Mr. Philips, as the recollection of the coffin cropped up in his mind. "He looks a dangerous vagabond, and I don't like that big stick he has in his hand."

"I say, old fellow, are you asleep?" broke in the rough voice of his persecutor. "What the devil are you dreaming about? I'd recommend you to join the Union, old lad, and then they won't burn your works as they've done your friend Gladstone's foundry."

"Mr. Gladstone is a very headstrong young man," said Mr. Philips, who fancied that a slight condemnation of his brother manufacturer might propitiate his mysterious companion. "I'm sure I've warned him often enough of the consequences if he persisted in such extreme measures."

"But he wouldn't be warned," retorted the other, striking his stick upon the battlements of a bridge, over which they were crossing, with a force that gave his companion a quickening palpitation of the heart for a week after. "I told him, myself, what would happen; and you see I was not out of my reckoning."

"I'm sure neither Mr. Young nor myself approved of all Mr. Gladstone did," cried Mr. Philips, in a deprecating tone; "but, my good man, you seem a decent fellow."

The man laughed sarcastically, as he seized hold of the bridle of Mr. Phillips' horse, crying out, as he threw her back upon her haunches—

"Get out of that, will you?"

"Get out of what?" demanded the manufacturer, struggling to keep his seat.

"Of all that blarney and humbug. You know well enough that I'm not a decent fellow, and that you're in a terrible funk lest I knock you off your horse and rob you where you stand. Eh! isn't that just it?"

"No! no! Upon my word of honour, I never harboured such a suspicion."

"Curse you, but you did; and by Jove I've half a mind to—"

"My dear fellow."

"What, at your blarney again, old boy? You appear to have learnt that thoroughly. Have you any more lies to the same tune?"

"Remember, sir, I'm a magistrate," said Mr. Philips, plucking up courage, as the man scowled upon him over his horse's neck. "This conduct is transportation, my man, at the very least."

"Bah! Who is here to transport me? There's nobody within a mile of us two. Now wasn't Gladstone's fire a grand one?"

Mr. Philips groaned as he admitted that it was.

" Philips' and Young's works will make a far finer illumination one of these nights if they don't take care what they're about. It's surprising how very inflammable factories are just now, old boy."

" Are they ?" gasped the manufacturer, with ludicrous helplessness.

" I'll be cursed if they're not. Why, they're regular volcanoes, and no mistake. Well, Mr. Philips, our roads part here," said he, as Mr. Philips' house appeared in view. " You've had warning, you know."

" Much obliged," stammered Mr. Philips, as gratefully as he had ever spoken for the largest order he had received. " Now, my man, do let go the bridle, will you ? I'll tell my partner what you've been saying about the Union, and you may depend upon a favourable answer."

" You can send it through the post, and tell the postman to be particular to give it into no other hands than mine, for fear that sneaking wretch, Gladstone, gets hold of it, eh ? Won't that do ? Isn't it a pity that the nights are not a bit darker ?"

" I don't understand."

" You old blockhead ! A fire's quite thrown away on these light nights. Suppose we put off firing your place till the winter."

" Ha ! he ! ha ! not so bad," exclaimed poor Philips, with a desperate attempt at jocularity. " Well, good-night, my friend."

" Stay, I'll open the gate for you," said the other, with mock politeness. " I dare say your bones are stiff."

And he held the gate open until Mr. Philips and his horse were half through, when he flung it back again and ran off with a loud laugh, stopping to listen, when he had gone about a hundred yards, to the noise the horse made as it gallopped over the well-kept gravel of Mr. Philips' carriage sweep.

" It would have been rare fun for Fanny," he said, with another loud laugh, as he walked on. " Hang it ! I wish I could make her laugh a bit, for what between fretting about home and crying her eyes out if I look the least cross, she's grown as ugly as the devil. What a confounded fool I was to hamper myself with her."

There was a ludicrous mixture of terror and self-importance in Mr. Philips' manner the next morning when he faced his brother manufacturers at Bradford, whither he went as soon after twelve o'clock as he decently could. They had met to determine what steps should be taken to search out and punish the miscreant who had fired William Gladstone's premises, as well as to determine what course should be pursued to save themselves against such another catastrophe. No one for a moment doubted that the fire was the work of an incendiary.

Mr. Philips got up and unburthened his mind of the perilous weight that oppressed it. In such goodly company he was wondrous bold, and even went the length of declaring a highwayman had attacked him, but that he had beaten him off, and had escaped, thanks to the fleetness of his horse. Browne sneered at this bravado, but the rest were all too panic-stricken to notice the discrepancy of his story.

" Has anybody seen Gladstone this morn-ing ?" some one demanded when Philips had finished. " We ought to know what he in-tends doing as soon as possible."

" I can tell you where he has been this morning, gentlemen," said Mr. Browne. "He has been making an affidavit before the magistrates, so as to spare you the trouble of ferretting out all the ins and outs of this busi-ness. You have nothing to do but to look to the safety of your own shops. But here he comes to speak for himself."

Mr. Gladstone came into the room at this moment, looking as quiet and self-possessed as if nothing had happened, and received the condolences of his brother manufactures as a matter of course. He had been before the magistrates, and the affair of the fire was already being investigated. He only hoped none of the gentlemen present would allow his misfortune to induce them to yield to the demands of the Union, but show a bold front, and the victory would assuredly be theirs before very long.

" Give me a grip of your hand, Gladstone," cried Browne, striding towards him when he had finished. " Dang it ! but thou'rt sterling metal, and I vastly like thy bull-dog courage."

" I'll never submit to be threatened, Mr. Browne," said William, returning his hearty grip.

" Did you hear of my being waylaid last night, Mr. Gladstone ?" said Mr. Philips, bustling up to him as he was leaving the room. " I was riding quietly home from your fire and, by Jove ! sir, a villain accosted me with the most diabolical threats of vengeance if I did not join the Union. Of course I don't intend, you know, but it shows what a vile set they are."

William smiled and said—

" There is not a doubt of that."

And, taking advantage of Mr. Philips going

off to detail his adventures to a new comer, he left the room and rode off home as quickly as he could.

As he proceeded towards Braidsworth he pulled up for a moment at a road-side well to allow his horse to drink, and so preoccupied was he with his own thoughts that he would not have noticed two men, who were lounging on the grassy bank beside it, had not an exclamation from one of the men attracted his attention.

" Are you making holiday to-day, Jobson ?" he said, rather surprised to discover that the speaker was Sarah Crisp's lover. " I thought you were more industrious than to do that."

" I've sprained my arm, sir," said Harry, who evidently did not wish to attract attention.

" He's a cursed ass that always works, Mr. Gladstone," said Harry's companion, with a kind of lawless impudence that attracted William's gaze to him in a moment. " This is a pleasant bank, sir, on a fine day."

"I have no doubt you find it so, my man," said Mr. Gladstone, who recollected in a moment that this man had made the most violent speech of the evening at the Union meeting the night Browne and himself went there, and without again speaking he turned his horse's head upon the road

"One or other of those men fired my foundry," muttered William, looking back at them, after he had ridden a hundred yards. "They are getting up, and going in the direction of Bradford. I'm sorry to see young Jobson in the leading strings of such a villanous scoundrel," and he rode on, his mind full of his losses and difficulties, only giving a thought at intervals to the two men whom he had seen leave the old well, and there rest in the pleasant sunshine.

If Uncle Newman would assist his nephew, all would yet be well, but without his aid William could scarcely expect to surmount his losses. He could not bear to borrow money of anyone else; but Mr. Newman was his relative, and he had often hinted that all he had would one day belong to his nephew and nieces; and surely he had a right to request the favour under the peculiar circumstances of the case.

But old Newman's character was so peculiar he felt anything but certain the favour would be acceded to him, and it needed all the stern self-reliance of his character to buoy him up under this uncertainty. If his uncle did help him he might get on again—if he did not, he would in all probability be a beggar.

All his deliberations ended in this, and an unpleasant ending it was.

He rode into the yard, and put the horse in the stable himself, and then walked through the kitchen, where Hannah was employed baking bread. The old servant lifted her eyes, and looked gravely at him, but her master set this gravity down to the score of the fire, and hurried on to the parlour.

"Oh! William! William!" exclaimed

Frances, bursting into tears, and flinging herself upon his neck as soon as he entered the room. " Oh! brother, how misfortunes gather around us!"

His heart sunk within him, as he put her gently into a chair, and asked what was the matter.

A fresh burst of grief was for a long time her only answer, but at last she sobbed out uncle Newman's name.

" He is dead—I know it all, Frances," exclaimed her brother, looking wildly into her pale face.

" No! no! Thank God, he still lives!" she cried, struggling to speak calmly; " there are a few lines from Sophia, which you had better read," and Frances handed him a crumpled note, which he had great difficulty in deciphering.

He learned from it that the old gentleman had been seized with a paralytic stroke, and was quite speechless at the time of her writing. That they had heard of William's

misfortune soon after midnight, and that
uncle Newman had been found in the sad
condition her letter described in the morning, and that either William or herself must
set out for Longford as soon as the note
reached them.

"Good God! Good God!" was the exclamation uttered in a harrowing voice by
William Gladstone, as soon as he had finished
the perusal of the note.

"My dear brother," said Frances, calming
herself with a great effort, "let me go to
Longford."

Her pale face looked most beautiful with
its earnest expression at this moment; and,
much as William was cast down by this fresh
sorrow, he could not forbear drawing her towards him and kissing her fair brow, as he
said—

"My dear sister, this must not be; poor
uncle Newman, if he be sensible, will expect
to see me, and everything else must give place
to my duty to him. I will be back by breakfast time to-morrow."

Frances felt he was right, and said nothing more, but hurried on the dinner as rapidly as possible to expedite his departure. The meal passed off in silence, for the hearts of both were too full to permit them to speak.

"If Alfred Vinen should call, Frances, tell him where I am gone," he said, as he mounted his horse. "Now, good-bye," and he rode off with a heavy heart.

CHAPTER III.

WILLIAM GLADSTONE had never before thought
the distance between Braidsworth and Longford so great as on this occasion; and he
spared neither whip nor spur to get there as
speedily as possible. An unwonted solemnity
seemed to brood over even the beautiful
gardens when he rode up to the house, as if in-
animate nature seemed mourning for the
owner of all the budding treasures of that
charming domain, and who was, alas ! soon to
exchange them for the silence of the grave.

He had been told by the sobbing woman
at the gate that Mr. Newman was still alive,
and the old gentleman's man-servant confirmed

the information when he met him in the hall.

" You must be prepared for a great change, Mr. Gladstone," he said, with grave significance, as he led him to his master's bedroom. " He's fearfully altered in the last twelve hours."

The blinds were drawn down to exclude the sun, giving to the chamber of the dying man that ghastly dimness that affects us so much on coming out of the bright daylight. Sophia was sitting at the head of the bed, pale and composed, watching the distorted face that had never been turned upon her but with the tenderest affection.

With feelings of the most solemn awe William approached his poor uncle, and, stooping down, kissed his forehead, on which death he saw was too surely stamped. The aged and withered face had lost much of the harshness that usually characterised it, and but for the distortion of the mouth looked almost as calm and placid as that of an infant.

" He has never spoken since we found him
in this wretched state, brother," whispered
Sophia shedding a few silent tears. "The
doctor says he will pass away in the state
you now see him."

" Was he much shocked on learning my
misfortune, Sophia?" asked William, who
could not restrain his own grief.

" Very much. The last word he uttered in
parting from me at night was to give you
his blessing. He was as gentle as a child
then."

" Poor, poor uncle!" murmured the
nephew. " It all seems like a horrible dream
to me."

"How are Frances and Kate?" Sophia
asked, after a long pause.

" Kate is still at 'Sunnyside.' Poor
Frances, of course, is sadly cut up under all
these misfortunes. She wished very much to
come to Longford in my place, but I would
not permit that, as I felt if our poor uncle
was conscious he would expect to see me."

"And the fire, brother; how did it happen?"
she asked.

"I have not the slightest doubt it was the
work of an incendiary. Everything was
safe when William Crisp left the place that
night."

"What a wicked, malicious action, William.
Someone belonging to the Union must have
done it."

"There is not the slightest doubt of that;
probably by the time I get back again the
miscreant will be known."

"I am afraid you are involved in a labyrinth
of trouble, William," said his sister, with a
heavy sigh. "Had you not better go down
stairs and get some refreshment?"

William could not eat, but he felt sick and
ill, and thought a breath of fresh air would
revive him, and he went down into the
garden, the sunny beauty of which contrasted
strangely with the silence and darkness of
the sick room. The first object almost that
he saw was his uncle's man, Jacob, leaning

over one of the fountains, whilst his gaze was fixed gloomily upon the distant landscape.

" Fine day, sir," he said, on seeing Mr. Gladstone, brushing his hard, horny hand across his eyes as he spoke.

" Very, Jacob," rejoined William, mournfully, " somehow I feel it almost too fine."

" And so do I, sir," said the other, bursting into tears. " I'd rather see the wildest storm that ever raged than all this beautiful sunlight just now. I never thought, sir, I'd see my old master laid aside in my time. We were boys together, Mr. Gladstone, and I feel somehow that I sha'n't be long after him."

The man turned and walked away, as if he was ashamed to let anyone see his grief, and William pursued his melancholy walk, wishing at times that he, too, could shake off this mortal coil, and thus escape the heart-breaking wretchedness that dogged him on every side, and then rallying as the natural hopefulness of his nature asserted its sway.

*   *   *   *

Uncle Newman passed away as gently as an infant breathing its last sigh on its mother's breast. Daylight had faded into night, and night in its turn had yielded to the dawn as those solemn watchers stood around his bed and witnessed his calm and peaceful departure.

As William drew up the blind, after all was over, the daylight fell cold and bright upon the wrinkled brow and glassy eyes which never again would gaze upon this lower world, in which his energetic yet humble spirit had played its part for three score years and ten. William kissed the clammy cheek ere covering it with the sheet, and then, with a hushed voice, told Sophia that they must both get a few hours' sleep if possible.

Poor Sophia was quite worn out, and suffered him to carry her to her chamber, and then he sought his own pillow, which he sorely needed after all the trying vicissitudes of the last four-and-twenty hours.

Sophia was still in bed when he started on his journey home some hours before noon, for he had a great deal to do at Braidsworth, and notwithstanding all the grief he felt for poor uncle Newman, it was absolutely requisite for his own credit that he should be on the spot to make those investigations which were so indispensably necessary in his circumstances.

He found Frances more nervous and more unhappy than he had remembered her for years, and he did not wonder at it, for no one understood his actual position better than herself.

" You need not tell me, brother," she said, sitting down beside him, " I can tell by your face that all is over."

And she burst into tears.

" Did he die quietly, brother ?" she asked, when she had become somewhat more composed.

" He went off like a lamb, Frances. Old

Jacob said he looked, before he died, just as he remembered him when they were both lads together."

" We ought to be very thankful he departed so easily, William. Sophia will be very ill after all these trials."

" I left her asleep in bed. Has Alfred Vinen been here to-day ?"

" Yes, he has," replied Frances, " but I was so painfully nervous and unhappy that I sent him away without seeing him."

" Well, my dear, I must go down to the foundry and see what can be saved from the wreck," he said, as cheerfully as he could. " I almost dread to look into things, I expect to find everything in such a total ruin."

" Matters may not be so bad as you anticipate, William. Ah ! if our poor uncle had lived."

" He would have helped me, you would have said, my dear. Well, God's will be done ! Thank God ! I can say that with humble faith. I have no doubt He sends

these trials now for our good. Good bye, for
the present," and he walked away with a firm
step.

Frances went and locked herself into her
room again and had a hearty cry. She possessed such a happy disposition that the
everyday cares of the world rarely affected
her at all, and she was on this account,
perhaps, more painfully moved by the deep
sorrow such as the present proved; and,
in addition to this, she had reason to dread,
from what had dropped from her brother, that
it was more than probable this sudden de-
struction of his property might cause him
great embarrassment in his business, if not
absolute ruin.

After a time, however, she began to feel
the folly of indulging her grief so morbidly.
If embarrassment had arisen the sooner it
was encountered the better; all the tears and
repinings in the world would not overcome
it, and with red eyes and pallid cheeks she
went about her household duties, determined

to steel her heart against indulging such dangerous feelings for the future.

William came home early in the afternoon, looking ill and unsettled, and evidently very much out of spirits. He had had a great many unpleasant things to do, during the forenoon, and they had proved, collectively, too much for his temper. He had, besides, a strange craving for sympathy, and Frances was not the person to give him what he yearned for in this novel state of feeling. He wanted something beyond even her, and he had determined in his own mind to go to ' Sunnyside' to find it. Perhaps a piece of information Alfred Vinen had given him in the morning, to the effect that Mr. Briscoe had gone back to Harrogate, had something to do with his determination in this matter. At all events he would go.

Frances' face flushed scarlet and then became very white when she began to discern, beneath the surface, the motive that prompted her brother to leave his business at such a time—especially when their oldest friend and only relative was still unburied— to go on such an errand. She did not then understand—and in fact she never learned from actual experience, for her own courtship long afterwards was singularly devoid of all the worst pangs and uncertainties of love—she did not understand, and was therefore unable to find a palliation for such a step; she could not believe that a man so immersed in business, and so matter-of-fact as her brother William, could do so very foolish and strange a thing as to ride all the way to 'Sunnyside' on this particular evening, merely to enquire after Miss Coulson's health.

She did not know that it is your matter-of-fact men who are sometimes by far the most romantic, and who do the most out-of-the-way actions, whenever the spirit of impulse moves them thereto; and she little suspected that beneath William's quiet exterior there slumbered a volcano which might one day lay waste the quieter nature that surrounded it with a hot

lava stream of passion that his most intimate
associate had never dreamed of his possess-
ing.

But she nevertheless had no thought of
preventing his going. She only looked grave
and sad, and said she supposed he would be
home early, for he looked fagged and ill; and
William promised he would attend to her
wishes in this respect, and set off, leaving
Frances with a dull, uneasy consciousness
that something was wrong either with her
brother or herself.

Mr. Gladstone's own feelings were the
strangest mixture it is possible to conceive.
First and foremost on the canvas of his brain
loomed, with terrible distinctness, this unfortunate fire, all the evil consequences of which
haunted his mind perpetually, forget them
how he might, for a moment or two, in some
sweeter dream of the fancy, that was blotted
out the next minute by the recurrence of
dark pictures even Agatha Coulson's sweet
face could not chase away. There was poor

uncle Newman, lying dead, with Sophia watching silently over him, and again Agatha's image arose, and he endeavoured to think entirely of her, when Mr. Briscoe would appear with his haughty face, as he had seen him on the day when his appearance had had such a visible effect upon Miss Coulson.

He tried to separate all these antagonistic fancies, but could not, for his brain was in that uneasy state, after long watching, when images crowd upon it in bewildering masses without the unhappy victim of their malice being able to make them vanish at his bidding, and when, like some unhappy necromancer, who has evoked a band of evil spirits whom he cannot control, he is perforce compelled to become an unwilling spectator of their mutinous *diablerie*.

All these ideas swept through his mind while he was approaching 'Sunnyside,' and by some strange affinity, for which it would perhaps be impossible to account, the nearer he drew to the residence of his mistress, the more palpable did her influence shew itself upon these waking reveries. By the time he had entered the Park he had worked himself into a very pretty rapture about her charms, recalling to his mind her graceful figure, her lovely face, with eyes humid with emotion; how the touch of her soft warm hand always thrilled him, as if an electric shock had swept through his system, and how pleasant were the tones of her low sweet voice to his ears, lingering on his charmed senses like the echoes of some exquisite melody long after the music itself has passed away.

The three girls Amelia, Kate, and Miss Coulson were sitting on a sort of rustic seat in the grounds as he rode up.

"I was sure you would come to-night, William," said Kate, springing up; "tell us all about that horrid fire—" and then she stopped suddenly, struck with his unusual gravity.

"Something much more serious than a fire has happened, Amelia," whispered Miss Coulson, equally struck with William's pale countenance, although she did not divine the cause.

"What is the matter, brother?" asked Kate, in a whisper.

"Uncle Newman is dead, my dear girl!" said he, kissing the soft cheek that was up-turned to his face.

"How sudden—how very sudden."

"Let us go away, Amelia, and leave them," whispered Agatha, with true wo-manly delicacy. "Come," and she began to steal away as if she had committed some great fault.

"Pray do not leave us, Miss Agatha," said Mr. Gladstone, coming up and holding out his hand with a manly confidence that became him admirably. "I have nothing to com-municate to Kate that you should not hear. She must know already that I am a ruined man!"

Kate's tears began to flow in silence as she took hold of his arm.

"Poor brother! poor uncle Newman!" burst from her lips.

"He died very easily, Kate," said her brother, with calm stoicism. "I don't think he suffered much."

"But you must have suffered, William," said she, with the intuitive delicacy of her sex, still keeping hold of his arm, and averting her face to hide her tears. "You were so hopeful, so happy in the morning, I remember."

"I was happy, Kate," rejoined he, with deep feeling. "Miss Coulson," turning to his fair young hostess, "did you ever know what it was to awake from some delicious dream to find yourself plunged in apparently hopeless grief?"

"Once, Mr. Gladstone, I experienced the sensation," she replied.

"Then you can pity my feelings when I arrived at Braidsworth and found my workshops in flames ! It was a frightful awakening, and enough of itself to crush any man; but when this—this sad affair comes on the head of it, I sometimes almost wonder that I am alive."

During this dialogue they had been walking towards the house, and it was a relief to all when they discovered Mrs. Coulson standing on the steps awaiting them.

"What can you be talking about, good folks, to make you walk so slowly," said she in her clear, sharp tones, as they came leisurely up. "My dear Mr. Gladstone, I am very sorry to hear of your misfortune."

"Thank you, madam," rejoined William, proudly.

"We saw the flames distinctly at 'Sunnyside', for the night was very dark and still. I can assure you, we were all disturbed, and Agatha, I'll answer for it, never slept a wink all night after."

Again Mr. Gladstone bowed his proud head, but this time his dark eye flashed, and a heightened colour spread itself over his pallid cheek.

" There was flame enough at any rate," said he quietly.

" I half thought of sending off the ' Sunny-side' engine at one time," said the good lady, who was growing more than usually loquacious, much to her daughter's uneasiness, " but Blewitt told me he was sure the fire would be extinguished long before they could get the lumbering old thing through our heavy cross-roads. And how is poor Miss Frances ?"

" Quite well, thank you."

" Well, that I'm sure is a comfort," said the good lady, who evidently thought people had no business to be well under such circumstances. " Pray, Agatha, ring the bell, and order some tea for Mr. Gladstone ; he looks sadly tired and out of spirits."

William thought he had a good right to be fagged and out of spirits, after all the sorrows and disasters of the last four-and-twenty hours, and very grateful he was for the strong tea Miss Coulson made him, and the adroit way in which she parried the inquisitive questions of her mother, whenever she saw, by his countenance, that the latter gave him pain.

" What has become of Kate all this time ?" asked the good lady, on discovering that she had left the room.

"She has a bad headache, I believe, mamma, and has gone to lie down."

" Kate is rather delicate," said Mrs Coulson, authoritatively. "I am sure, Mr. Gladstone, your Braidsworth air does not suit her."

William smiled, and said he was sorry to hear it, but of course Mrs. Coulson knew best.

" She shall take plenty of riding exercise whilst she is with me," said Mrs. Coulson. " I'm sure it would be quite a kindness to those two ponies, Agatha, for they are getting far too fat."

"Blewitt probably feeds them too well, mamma," suggested her daughter, laughing.

"Nonsense, my dear; they are dying for want of exercise. Amelia, dear, I will send Blewitt into Braidsworth to-morrow for your riding habit."

"There is really no necessity, mamma," said her daughter, "I have two, and we cannot all ride at the same time."

"Your habits won't fit Miss Vinen, my love," said the old lady, peering at Amelia through her spectacles. "Mr. Gladstone, is your cup empty?"

Agatha blushed to find that it was, and was busily engaged in replenishing it, when Mrs. Coulson again began with—

"I have had a letter from Mr. Banks to-day, my love," addressing her daughter, "saying that he will be here to-morrow with your poor dear father's solicitor, to make some arrangements about re-letting the home farm and the woodlands."

"Very well, madam," said Miss Coulson, carelessly, "need I stay at home to meet him?"

" Well, I think, my love, you had better ; you know Mr. Banks always makes a point of your being present on these occasions."

" I wish he had put it off for a time," said her daughter, in no very pleasant tone. " No one I am sure is so plagued with troublesome tenants as I am."

" You ought to be very thankful you have them, my love," said Mrs. Coulson. " Blewitt says there is not such clover in the whole county as that on the home farm."

Miss Coulson's manner betrayed the consciousness she felt that all this was but a foolish parade, on the part of her mother, of her landed possessions, and she looked vexed and uneasy ; and more than once half arose from her seat as if she wanted something.

" What do you want, love ? More toast did you say ? Stay, I will ring the bell," and Mrs. Coulson took the bell-rope in her hand.

" There is an abundance of toast upon the table," said her daughter.

" But it must be cold by this time, my dear—Mr. Gladstone, another cup ?"

" Nothing more, my dear madam," said William, receding from the table.

" Now, Agatha, you had better go and see poor Kate, and take Amelia with you. Mr. Gladstone can sit and bear me company during your absence."

William felt anything but grateful for the privilege. He had much rather that Mrs. Coulson had herself gone to look after his sister and left Agatha with him in the interval; and on Miss Coulson rising to leave the room, he also arose from his chair.

" Going already, Mr. Gladstone ?" was the old lady's first exclamation, as he held out his hand and said good night. " You surely cannot be in earnest."

" Frances begged me to be home early," he said, " and I promised her I would; my unpopularity makes it politic that I should not travel after dark."

"But it will be light as day till eleven o'clock; the moon shines so brightly."

"I am glad to hear it; I shall be home by daylight."

"You have scarcely sat down in my house, sir; this is not using an old friend well."

"I was with you all day yesterday, my dear madam. Only consider for a moment what would be your feelings if you were told I had been shot in returning, through your detention," and he smiled.

"What nonsense you talk! Nothing but your inordinate vanity would prompt you to anticipate such a fate," retorted Mrs. Coulson.

"I really must go. Would you enquire if my sister has any message for Frances?"

Seeing that he was determined to go, Mrs. Coulson went to make the enquiry, and William, sitting down again, took out his letters, glanced at the superscriptions, put some into his pocket again unopened, and read the rest. So leisurely did he do this, and so calm and determined did he look when the task was done, that a looker-on would have felt assured that their contents were all in the ordinary routine of business, and scarcely required a second thought.

Miss Coulson came in with Kate's love, and some trifling message to Frances, which long afterwards she found to have been accurately delivered.

"I am deeply in your debt," said he, as he took Miss Coulson's warm, trembling hand in his cool, hard palm. "Some day, it may be, I may return it."

And with a pleasant smile he took his leave.

"What a fine noble fellow he is," thought Agatha, watching him from the window, "without being handsome, how his clear, sharp-cut features enchain the eye, and what a manly courage lurks beneath that quiet modesty."

CHAPTER IV.

EVERY one in Braidsworth the following morning knew that William Gladstone had failed.
The Rector's butler heard it at the bar of the
Green Dragon, and the Rector himself heard
it from his clerk.   Henry Salmon went up to
his brother-in-law Crisp's to break it to poor
William, who was confined to his bed with
fever, and went away with his errand untold
when he found him raving in bed, and his
poor, more than half dead wife sitting holding him up in her arms.   There was misery
enough there without his sad news to increase
it.

William Gladstone had failed! It was worse than either the fire or the fever, bad as both were. Every one said the latter could not last long now, although there were fresh cases every day, and those that were ill seemed to mend but slowly, or not at all. Everyone had hoped that the fire would prove but a temporary disaster, and that the Braidsworth Works would soon get into working order again, for the village seemed quite dead without the clang of William's forge hammers; now all these hopes were doomed to be disappointed.

Towards the middle of the day it began to be whispered about that it was owing to some great failure at Halifax that this misfortune had come to pass. Mr. Gladstone had received letters from the firm the day before, announcing their suspension at a time when their credit stood unusually high, and it was said his losses amounted to many thousands. "It was a rare stiff sum that, and enough to break anybody's back, let alone a man struggling with such heavy misfortunes as he was doing."

"It is better that it should come now, Frances," said her brother, calmly, as they sat alone together late in the night. " Moore and Halfield's dishonoured bill is considerably above four thousand pounds. Curse them ! I thought they could never fail. There are others to follow. I will call a meeting of my creditors to-morrow, and lay the state of my affairs before them. Thank God ! all my poor workmen have been paid every penny. I don't think, sister, they will wish to put me into jail, at any rate."

" God forbid they should, William; you have done nothing wrong."

"I am not the less punishable on that account, Frances. Our glorious laws treat the unfortunate and the criminal pretty much the same in that respect. My creditors, however, are all honorable men, and would scorn to strike a fallen fellow-creature. We must remove into Bradford as soon as it is all over."

" Because you can get employment there, William ?"

" Exactly so. We will let this dear old place. How fortunate, Frances, that our cautious fáther settled it upon his daughters, rather than on his unfortunate son. We will take a small house somewhere in the suburbs of the town. Poor Sophia will feel the change keenly."

" I do not think she will, William. Did you know I had some conversation yesterday, with Dr. Vinen."

" How should I ? What, pray, was the topic ?"

" Very nearly allied to what we are talking about. I was telling him I wished to commence a school."

" A school ! You silly fool !"

" A school, William. Don't you think the young women of the present day incur a heavy sin by the almost systematic idleness in which they indulge? Just call to mind the many families, in our own limited circle, in which the young women are living upon the industry of their fathers, and—and—"

" Brothers ! you would say.   Well ?"

" Yes, and brothers," continued Frances, looking affectionately at William. " Why is this ?   Because they are too proud, or too in-dolent to work to get their own living. Wasting the best years of their lives simply because it is the fashion to do so.   They may never marry, because they may never have the chance, and yet they live on in idleness.   Did God create women to be such worthless en-cumberers of the earth !   How I should detest such a fate !"

Frances became quite excited, and almost talked herself out of breath, so her brother continued the subject.

" You are quite right, Frances.   It is both wrong and wicked, and where such a charge falls upon a brother, it is very shameful—but about the school."

" We must all set about working in right earnest now, William, everyone trying to give you a helping hand to regain your former position—Kate must be housekeeper and wait on Sophia; I will try my best to bring as much grist to the mill as I possibly can."

"If you can get pupils."

"I have no doubt of that. Dr. Vinen has promised me his support, and you know what influence he possesses."

"You are a brave, good girl, Frances," said her brother, smiling; "and how long, may I ask, has this clever scheme been hatching in your wise head?"

"For many months, William : ever since you began to look sad."

"Did I ever look sad?"

"I noticed it coming on twelve months ago, though I dare say no one else did."

"And what induced you to think so?"

"Because, one day, when some gentlemen were dining here they talked about the dullness of trade, and I could not help noticing the expression that, for a moment, passed over your countenance when the observation was made. That little circumstance induced me to think of some plan by which I might aid you."

"But, my dear girl, such an employment is beneath you," said William, wishing to discover how far she was sincere in what she said.

"Beneath me!" echoed Frances.

"Yes, beneath you."

"It is not. I shall be proud of it."

"Can you bear the neglect of your former fine friends, when they find you transformed into a female pedagogue?"

"They will not be worth a moment's consideration, if their friendship cannot stand such a trial," said Frances, proudly.

"You will find it a very wearisome employment, Frances."

"Not more so than many others; a clerk's for instance."

"Besides, schoolmistresses are so badly paid."

"Perhaps so. I must look at the brighter side, and contend with and conquer these difficulties; I do hope, dear brother, you will refrain from throwing unnecessary impediments in my way."

William was satisfied. He saw that his sister was in earnest, and her scheme had no further opposition from him.

" I am very thankful uncle Newman was spared the grief of hearing of my failure," said William, changing the conversation; " thank God, he died in ignorance of that."

" That is some alleviation, William, now that he is taken from us," said Frances, earnestly. " Earthly sorrows and earthly cares will never trouble his now happy spirit more. Come, brother, it is time you were in bed," and she lighted the candle.

Her calmness and self-possession, at a time when most women would have been either thoroughly crushed or overwhelmed with grief, quite surprised her brother. Instead of indulging in vain, useless lamentations over his misfortunes, she set herself resolutely to the task of assisting him to reconstruct his fallen fortunes, and although these were at a very low ebb, yet both were sanguine enough to hope that a day of prosperity might sooner or later dawn upon them again.

Captain Vinen called at "The Rookery" the next morning whilst William and his sister were at breakfast, and his warm, manly greeting on entering the room did them more good than all the whining sympathy in the world could have accomplished.

"I am sorry to hear, Gladstone, your fire is not to be your only trial," said he, with a sailor-like frankness, after he had declined a cup of coffee. "It would be false delicacy in me to affect ignorance of what has happened, when every man, woman, and child in Braidsworth knows it."

"There is no necessity to blush for our misfortunes," said William, with his usual quiet smile; "my failure was a disaster as unexpected as it was sudden."

"If a thousand or so would be of any assistance," said their guest, with the delicacy of a high-toned mind, "I am sure it is heartily at your service."

"You could not offer it more heartily than I would take it," said William, grasping his hand. "I regret to say my losses are too heavy to allow me to accept your generous offer, and the only course open to me consists in giving up everything I possess to my creditors. The poor honest fellows whom I employed, will, I fear, suffer severely for a time."

"We must all try to alleviate their distress as much as possible," said the Captain, energetically. "Fever, and fire, and famine are enough to desolate any Eden, and Braidsworth never was that. Dr. Smith says the pestilence is daily gaining ground, and my father talks of having a day set apart for humiliation and fasting in consequence."

"Hannah told me this morning," said Frances, in her low, soft voice, "that poor William Crisp has caught the fever, and is very ill."

"I will go down at once to see him," said

her brother, looking for his hat. "Alfred, will you walk that way with me?"

"Yes, I shall be very happy to do so," replied the Captain.

"I have mislaid my gloves," said William, "excuse my leaving you for a minute," and he went out of the room.

Captain Vinen walked to the window, and leaning against the shutter, watched Frances arranging her flowers.

"I wish, Miss Frances, you would persuade your brother to take that money," said he, bluntly. "I have no earthly use for it myself, and I am sure it would be of service to him at this time."

"William feels your generosity deeply, Captain Vinen," said Frances, whose little white hand trembled as she held the vase in which she was arranging the flowers. "No one, I am certain, could appreciate your kind offer more than my brother does; and nothing but the utter hopelessness of his affairs would prevent him accepting it."

"I am sorry, Miss Frances, I am such

a poor devil that it is all I have to offer," said he. " Our naval service offers but few chances of acquiring wealth."

" It confers something much nobler," said Frances, turning round, and fixing her searching eyes upon him.

" I know what you mean, well enough," said he, with a bitter smile, " and certainly fame is a very pretty toy to amuse oneself with, but at this moment a few rolls of bank notes would be much more to the purpose, Miss Frances."

" They undoubtedly would," rejoined Frances, with a smile at his vehemence, " but, as they cannot be had, we must put up with the want of them in the best way we can."

" How coolly you take matters," said the Captain, looking at her in some surprise. " Do you know what a failure means ?"

" I think I do; it is a misfortune that no honourable mind would stoop to if there were any chance of escape from it; and in my brother's case there is none."

He sat down in a chair, and pulled his hat over his eyes, as if tired of arguing. Frances from where she stood could see his mouth writhe and his colour change from red to white, as if he was deeply moved.

"You seem to bear this misfortune better than some of your friends do, Miss Frances," said he at last, in a low voice. "I expected to find you, at least, in deep distress."

"I am glad you are disappointed. If I am not happy under my brother's misfortunes, I am at least calm and hopeful," said Frances, quietly. "William's losses might happen to any honourable man, and why should he be exempt from the ordinary chances and changes of life. We intend letting this house when William's affairs are all settled, and removing into Bradford."

"Into Bradford!" he exclaimed, staring at her in some dismay, "into that smoky hole?"

"Yes," said his companion, not in the slightest degree dismayed, "I expect we shall

live very comfortably there, despite all incon-
veniences. It was my idea."

" And the last idea I should have imagined
you would have entertained," he said, thoughtfully. " I suppose it is for William's con-
venience ?"

" Yes it is. He intends accepting a situation in one of the large iron-works near the
town."

" I shall see you all looking as white as
ghosts, the next time I take a run over to
poor old Braidsworth," said he, talking quickly,
as he always did when he was vexed, " but I
suppose it is no use arguing with you ?"

" Not the least in the world, Captain Vinen,
you know I never change my mind when it is
once made up."

Captain Vinen knew she did not, and said
something to that effect. Frances had never
seen him so unmanageable before. He was
usually so agreeable and courteous, that his
present spirit of contradiction sat badly upon
him. The fact is he had talked himself into

a passion, when he found Frances as untract-
able as her brother, on a point on which he
had set his heart. After a time he said—

"I'm a rash, headstrong fool, Miss Frances.
Is it not the worst possible taste to try to
thrust a kindness down people's throats when
they cannot swallow it ?"

Frances acquiesced in this sage observation,
with a smile, and said—

"It may be foolish; but I am sure your
intention is everything that is kind."

"But what about this Bradford scheme ?"
said he. "You don't intend to bury your-
selves alive in some dismal den."

"We shall take the best and most cheerful
house we can afford," said Frances, with a
business-like air. "Sophia, you know, requires it."

He thought that some one else did, but did
not say so. Frances was much more precious
to him than Sophia, and his jealous anxiety
had already painted her pining away in some
smoky, dull, street. How he cursed his

poverty, for preventing his offering her a home, such as he thought she deserved, and yet he felt it would be madness to link her destiny with his own uncertain fortunes, for years to come, perhaps.

Fortunately William came back at that moment, and interrupted their tête-à-tête, much to his sister's relief. Grateful as she was to Captain Vinen for his generous offer, she could not but feel annoyed at the pertinacity with which he combatted the future arrangements of her brother and herself, which were unquestionably the best they could make under existing circumstances; and it was certainly very provoking to meet opposition from such a quarter just then.

" Your sister tells me you are going to live in Bradford," said the Captain, as they walked through the village to William Crisp's house.

" Yes, we have decided on that," said Mr. Gladstone, drily ; " and Frances intends taking pupils."

"Your sister intends commencing a school!"
he cried.

"The project, I believe, emanated from
your father."

"Don't you feel that such an employment is
rather a degrading one, Gladstone, for such a
girl?"

"Not in the least, or your father would not
have advised her to such a step. The next
time you come to see us you will find her
prim, precise, and methodical, as all school-
mistresses are, in the midst of her little world,
distributing birch and spelling with a liberal
hand."

The picture appeared anything but a pleasing one to his companion, who walked on
without speaking for some distance.

"I wish, William," he said, at last, "you
would take that money; it's of no use in the
world to me."

"Thank you, Alfred. It would be of still
less to me. Hard work is what I have to look
forward to for some time to come."

"But something advantageous might turn up, when a little ready money might be of service to you."

"I can always write to you if anything of the kind should happen. There's poor Crisp's house."

The blind was drawn down; but that might be by chance. Mr. Gladstone opened the door gently and entered the little kitchen. Mrs. Salmon, Crisp's sister, was sitting near the fire busy knitting. Hearing some one enter she looked up, and saluted Mr. Gladstone with a sad "good morning."

"We have come to inquire after your brother, Mrs. Salmon," said William, kindly. "I hope he is not very ill."

"Not now, sir," said Mrs. Salmon; "if you step this way, sir, you can see both him and the mistress."

And she led the way up the dark and narrow stairs.

The blind of the window in William Crisp's room was down, and Mrs. Salmon, going to the window, drew it up and admitted the sunlight into the small but neat chamber. Then she sat down on the window seat and burst into a passionate flood of tears, for William Crisp and his wife lay side by side on the bed attired in the simple garments of the grave, the wife's arm thrown partly on the breast of her companion.

"She died first, the dear angel," sobbed Bessy Salmon, as Mr. Gladstone went to the bed, and placed his hand gently on the cold cheek of his humble friend. "Oh! Mr. Gladstone, isn't this a fearful judgment? It was not the fever that killed them; they both died of a broken heart, sir."

Mr. Gladstone's heart throbbed wildly as he stood looking on that sad sight. At that moment he felt as if he would gladly die himself, so intense was the misery he suffered on seeing this fresh addition to his troubles. He staggered to a chair—sat down, burying his face in his hands—and suffered his tears to flow unchecked.

"She had an easier death than poor William," said Bessy, in her quiet grief. "Eh! his was a weary flitting, for his spirit was sore grieved for the bairns, poor things. 'Bessy, Bessy,' he was always crying, 'don't forsake them;' and then he would take his wife's cold hand in his and kiss it, and cry out again; then he would utter a prayer when he was freer from pain, and entreat his Maker to be a Father to them, in such a way that it quite melted one's heart to hear him. He often mentioned you, sir, and said how good you were. Then he would mutter something about poor Harry Jobson, which we couldn't understand, and so he went off."

"Where is Sarah?" asked William, kindly.

"Down at our house, sir. Poor thing, she went out of one fainting fit into another, when she discovered that both her father and mother were dead. It's an awful thing, Mr. Gladstone, to see husband and wife lying side by side in that way."

William turned his head away—he was

struggling hard with his own grief—and allowed the poor woman to go on unchecked.

" It was a great relief to poor William that he died out of debt," she said, wiping her eyes with the corner of her apron. " He always had a horror of owing anybody a farthing, and there is a trifle left in the cupboard after all."

" I will be at the expense of the funeral, Mrs. Salmon," said Mr. Gladstone, placing his purse beside her on the table. " I owe poor William much more than I can ever repay."

She returned the purse with a prouder gesture than he could have expected from her, with the remark that the funeral money was already provided from another quarter.

" But the family may require it," said William, in a gentle tone.

" Thank you kindly, sir; but I cannot take it, and him lying there still in the house. He never took a penny in all his life that he did not earn by the sweat of his brow; and I cannot, indeed I cannot, take it."

Mr. Gladstone did not press her further, much as he felt it must be needed, and with one more look at poor Crisp and his insensible partner he followed Captain Vinen down the narrow stairs, and passed out into the street.

"How sad and silent the street seems," he said, in a feeble voice, on remembering that it was the time when the workmen were generally hurrying to their dinners. "The very walls seem as if they bore a curse upon them, Alfred. I suppose you know they have taken up young Jobson, on suspicion of setting fire to my foundry?"

"Amelia told me about it this morning at breakfast. He is a lover, I believe, of poor Crisp's daughter."

"I suppose so. He is a violent Unionist, and that, coupled with his being seen coming past the factory shortly before the fire was discovered, has induced the suspicion against him. I saw him sitting by the roadside in company with the prime agitator of all the mischief, a scoundrel of the name of Smooth."

"Ah! It is through the specious urging of such vile fellows, that the poor working-men are brought into trouble and induced to join in the strikes, without reflecting that these agitators are well paid and well fed, whilst their dupes starve."

"Quite true," rejoined his companion, "but the mischief does not end with the injury to the workmen, for their wives and children suffer at the same time."

"It's a pity the law doesn't lay hold of those firebrands. I hope Smooth has been arrested, as well as Jobson."

"I am sorry to say he has not. He has already disappeared, and Jobson, guilty or innocent, is left to bear the brunt of the offence."

"What sort of character does Jobson bear?" asked Captain Vinen, with some slight curiosity.

" We can bring no fault against him," said William, who had nothing whatever to do with Jobson's arrest. " He has always borne an irreproachable character, and has been a most exemplary son to his honest, widowed mother, and, until very recently, a hard-working, industrious lad. The very fact of his intimacy with that villanous instigator, Smooth, will condemn him if committed for trial."

" He must be tried, I should think," said the Captain, in his matter-of-fact way. " It will be a terrible thing for his poor mother."

" She is a woman of great strength of mind, with very decided religious feelings, and she bears up wonderfully under the infliction. I am more sorry for poor Sarah Crisp, who has trouble enough already, without this addition. If I can save him, I will do so, for I have no doubt in my own mind of his innocence, ugly as appearances are against him. Good-bye for the present."

CHAPTER V.

THE oldest inhabitant in Braidsworth could not remember such an assemblage of people —old, young, and middle-aged,—as that which accompanied William and Mary Crisp to the grave. People came from the neighbouring villages and towns to see them laid in the ground, for William's fearless, and upright character was known and appreciated in the whole neighbourhood, and many a dark cheek looked pale, many a stern eye moistened when Dr. Vinen's voice was heard, in the solemn stillness that reigned around him, uttering the mournful words "Earth to earth! dust to dust! ashes to ashes!"

As the earth rattled on the coffins, those

who had leisure to observe what was passing noticed that a tall, slight youth, whose pale, sad face was relieved only by the plainness of its other features, and the restless fire that burned in his large full eyes, stole one arm round the weeping girl that stood at his side, and whispered something in her ear, which seemed only to increase the vehemence of her grief, if that, indeed, was possible.

He was one of the group gathered round the clergyman, and this of itself marked him out as belonging to the family of the deceased. A fresh-faced country-looking man stood next him, appearing as sorrowful and wretched as his plump, jovial face and well-fed figure, respectably attired in black, permitted him ; and yet, he probably took poor Mary's death quite as much to heart as either Henry Salmon or his buxom wife, although both of them shed tears plentifully enough, whereas not a single tear rolled down his ruddy cheek, nor a sigh broke from his sorrowing breast.

The youth, however, several times passed his hand across his eyes, and held his hat so that the flowing crape, with which it was bound, in a great measure concealed his pale intelligent features from the lookers-on. When all was over, he still kept close to his weeping companion, supporting, rather than leading her from the churchyard, for her grief was so excessive that she seemed incapable of walking without his aid.

He scarcely spoke during their progress to the house which death had desolated so fearfully, whilst his companion's tears flowed on unchecked.

"We munnot stay long here, Robert; the place sends a cold shudder all through me," whispered the country-looking man, as they sat down in the kitchen along with Henry Salmon and the neighbours who had been specially invited.

"We'll go, father, the moment poor Sarah is ready," rejoined the youth, with more decision than one would have expected from his physiognomy. "Poor girl, she sadly needs rest !"

"Yes, yes, that's quite right, Bob," continued the other, shivering ; "but this place makes me feel quite ill-like. It's but a poor house, although thy aunt did live in it, and—"

"Hush, father ! You can tell me all about that when we get home again," rejoined the son, moving away. "Mrs. Salmon, don't you think my cousin had better lie down for a short time ?"

Sarah was laid as pale, and almost as cold, as marble on her bed, holding her aching head between her hands, and trying to recall her mind to the extent of her misfortunes. She had almost forgotten Harry Jobson's disgrace in the fresher and bitterer loss that had befallen her in the death of her parents ; and yet, at times, a dim recollection of that event, which would have been considered a heavy affliction at any other time, flitted across her brain, adding fresh force to the tears she shed for the dead.

"Robert Fisher insists on your drinking

this nice hot tea, my dear lass," said Mrs. Salmon, entering the room with a small tray in her hand. " Come, Sarah, darling, sit up and drink it; I'm sure it will do you a world of good."

Sarah stared at her as if she did not comprehend what she said, her pale face and rigid expression of features betraying the depth of her grief, which, from the absence of her two brothers, she had to indulge without the sweet privilege of sharing it with others.

Although a kind-hearted woman, Mrs. Salmon possessed but little delicacy of feeling, as her next speech testified.

" You mustn't lie there, lass, crying thy eyes out in that fashion, for I know very well that thy uncle Fisher won't sit long in the kitchen."

"Oh! aunt Bessie, my heart will break," sobbed poor Sarah, as a fresh outburst of tears coursed down her cheeks. " I cannot go to Chilworth to-day with Uncle Fisher and Robert."

" Thoul't be obliged to go, my lass," said Mrs. Salmon, sitting down at the side of the bed, " there's thy uncle's cart coming down the street, so thou'd better drink the tea before Robert comes to seek thee."

" He might let me remain one night in the house after they have been carried out of it, aunt Bessie," said Sarah, sitting up and laying her thin white face on her companion's shoulder. " Only one night."

" Stuff, Sarah, thy wits are wandering," said Bessie Salmon, losing all patience, " get on thy cloak and bonnet this minute."

Contrary to her expectation, Sarah arose from the bed, and without another word put on her black bonnet and cloak.

" Now I'm ready," said she, and opening the door she went down stairs, where the funeral guests sat decorously sad round the room.

" Good bye for a time, uncle Henry," said she, going up to Henry Salmon and pressing his hands in her cold grasp.

" Good bye, dear Sarah," was his rejoinder, as he kissed her white forehead, "the mistress and me will be out to see thee before long."

" Thou can sit inside with thy cousin, Robert, and—I will drive," whispered Uncle Fisher to his son. " I can't talk so that she will understand me, and so I'd rather be on the shafts."

" Poor thing, I don't think she's fit for talking much," said Robert, glancing at Sarah's weary expression of countenance. " However, you can sit where you like, father," and without noticing the company further, Mr. Fisher went out and pretended to busy himself with the horse and cart.

Robert, in the meantime, took leave of the rest of the company, and then giving his hand to Sarah, led her to the door, where a small covered cart, with red curtains at the back and sides, drawn by an active pony, was standing.

Uncle Fisher had already taken his seat on the shaft, and was now casting many an impatient look from his elevated position upon the little group that had gathered together to witness their departure.

They were fairly off at last, although as long as the village remained in sight the pony proceeded at a very slow pace, but once the open country fairly gained uncle Fisher began to display his skill as a charioteer, and the little pony soon mended its pace to a trot, for the cart was very light of itself, and neither Robert nor Sarah added much to its weight.

The sun was just setting as they approached Chilworth, a pretty village with houses scattered very much at random down the side of a steep hill. The place looked cool and pleasant, with the woods lying around it in all directions, whilst a rapid stream, the beauty of which was not marred by the weirs and locks that retarded its progress lower down, gave a life and animation to the picture that made it all but perfect in Robert Fisher's critical eyes.

" There's Bobby and Tommy standing at

our door, Sarah," said he, as a turn of the road brought Mr. Fisher's house into view, and at the words his companion looked up and recognised, in the two black figures running at that moment from the stack-yard, the only two relatives she had in the world.

"Come! come! don't stand kissing and hugging here in the road, but get into the house, my lassie," cried uncle Fisher, with a rough sort of kindness. " Helen, woman! what's gotten thee that ye don't come forward to welcome Sarah to Chilworth?"

" Thou's always in such a hurry, master," retorted Mrs. Fisher, bustling forward with her sleeves tucked high up her plump rosy arms, for she had been in the dairy. " My bonnie bairn, I'm glad to see thee," she continued, taking her niece in her arms and giving her a smacking kiss on both cheeks. " I've had the tea put back this half hour or more, waiting your coming. Don't you think Tommy grown stouter than he was, and the little rogue has got such a colour!"

So she chatted on in her hearty kindly way, striving to cheer the pale sorrowful girl, who was sitting beside her with a hand of each brother clasped in her own; then scolding Robert and his father by turns, arranging the tea things on the small round table, buttering the cakes, and making the tea with the pleasant bustle and importance that all thoroughly clever housekeepers love to assume on these occasions.

She was equally stout and comfortable-looking as her husband, with a pleasant, roguish eye, a face all dimpled over with smiles and blushes, and a hearty voice that had a kind of music of its own which made you love to listen to it, even when nothing more profound than Bob's last tumble into the pond behind the house was under discussion.

Looking round the cosy kitchen, radiant with the western sunbeams, with the sides of bacon on its walls, and the well-kept shining walnut-tree presses, through the half opened doors of which you caught a glimpse of Mrs.

Fisher's gold and white china and glass, no wonder Mr. Fisher should have felt the contrast of poor William's dark, mean kitchen so keenly as he did.

Charles Fisher, in fact, was a substantial, thriving yeoman, who had gathered about him all the comforts of his class. The house itself was rather pinched for room, but still there was a spare bed-room, with a neat Kidderminster carpet on the floor, a mahogany bedstead, hung with white dimity curtains, a rather small dressing table, on which,—in addition to a swing looking-glass—laid Mrs. Fisher's Bible and hymn book, with a spray of lavender put in at the chapter she had last read.

On the opposite side of the kitchen was the only sitting-room in the house, which, simply as it was furnished, was always gay and pleasant looking, with greenhouse plants that blossomed as finely in the window as if they had been in a first rate greenhouse. Mr. Fisher's wealth, in truth, lay in his fold yard and stack yard, and these, reader, you shall be invited to inspect some fine afternoon, to see his lazy oxen, prize pigs, and sleak horses.

Robert was his only child, and being of rather delicate health and somewhat spoilt as well, was permitted to do pretty much as he pleased. The youth's pleasure was to be an artist, partly because he had a rambling disposition, partly because it was a fair excuse for him to see more of the world than the circumscribed limits of Chilworth permitted, and partly because he really loved the art, and sketched admirably for one so young.

"Thou looks't sorely tired, Sarah," said Mrs. Fisher, towards the close of her first evening at Chilworth; "would you like to go to bed, my love?"

"I should, aunt, very much; I am quite worn out."

"Thous't not had thy supper yet, my lass," said Mr. Fisher, hospitably. "Sit down a bit till Robert comes in, and we'll have it directly."

"I cannot eat," rejoined Sarah, forcing a

smile. "You know, uncle, I've gone through a great deal to-day, and—"

"That thou hast, my lass, and thoul't need the bed after it."

Mr. Fisher kissed his niece, and allowed her to depart in peace to her repose.

"We shall all be in bed very soon, Sarah," said Mrs. Fisher, when she and her niece had gained the spare bed-room.

"Do you always go to bed so early, aunt?" asked Sarah.

"Bless you, my dear, your uncle is very often in bed and fast asleep by eight o'clock at night."

"And what time does uncle rise in the morning?"

"In summer time he is never in bed much after four."

This was very different to the hours Sarah had been accustomed to, but she wisely re-solved to conform to the Chilworth ways as long as she remained there.

"Bobby and Tommy are always off to the

pastures with the men by five every morning," continued Mrs. Fisher, as she turned down the bed clothes. "I wish Robert would get up as early."

"Is my cousin not an early riser?" asked Sarah.

"Sometimes he does, but it's only by fits and starts, and that only vexes your uncle instead of pleasing him, for he says the lad never gets up unless he's got one of his sketching fits in his brain. He'll be glad of your company these long summer days, if you would like to wander about with him hunting about for beautiful scenery."

Sarah was too unhappy just then to permit her to anticipate much pleasure from this announcement, so she merely acquiesced by saying—

"Thank you, aunt."

"My good man always blames me," went on Mrs. Fisher, "for Robert's idleness, but what can I do? He is our only child, and I cannot find it in my heart to contradict the lad's fancies. If he should die what value would all our money be to us. I always tell Charles so when he grumbles about it. Thank God we've enough for all."

" She's a canny bit thing, Helen," said her husband, on her return to the kitchen, just before supper time.

" She's the very picture of your sister, Charles," was Mrs. Fisher's reply. " I couldn't help looking at her as she lay with her thin white face on the pillow, the likeness was so striking. Whatever can have become of Robert to keep him out till this hour ?"

" That lad gets worse and worse," said his father, good humouredly ; " he'll never make a farmer."

" Then the best way is not to try to make him one, Charles," rejoined Mrs. Fisher, with much earnestness ; " we have enough for both him and ourselves."

" It would break my heart, Helen," said

her husband, with a deep sigh, " if this bit homestead should ever pass from the Fishers after I'm dead and gone."

" Mayhap it won't. Robert can live here just as well as anywhere else," said the indulgent mother, stifling her own pain, and speaking in the pleasant, hopeful way she was accustomed. " I'm certain he loves that snug bed-room of his, all hung round with the sketches he has made of the fold-yard, and the woods down by the water side, far too dearly to dream for a moment of ever leaving them all."

" He is now coming through the stack-yard," said Mr. Fisher, as Robert's figure was seen advancing to the house as his father had indicated; " and he takes no notice whatever of that bonny polled heifer standing close beside him. Why Bobby and Tommy know more about her weight than he does."

It was only to his wife that Mr. Fisher ventured to complain in this way, for Robert, in reality, ruled his father just as effectually as he did his mother. He came into the kitchen whistling a tune, a sure sign that he was in the best of humours.

"Is supper ready, mother?" he asked, as soon as he had seated himself.

"It will be directly, Robert. Sarah has gone to bed."

Robert received this piece of information very graciously, adding that he thought she looked very ill, and he hoped a night's rest would do her good.

"Will you go to Halifax with me, to-morrow, Robert?" asked his father. "It's market day."

"Yes, I want some colours sadly, father. I couldn't finish the sky in a sketch I was making, for want of some ultramarine. I'll get that worsted for you, too, mother, if you'll give me the shade you want?"

"You'll have to rise with the lark, my lad," said his father, significantly.

"That's easily managed," rejoined the son,

with a peculiar smile, " mother can call me
when she gets up to have your breakfast
ready."

They were up and away when Sarah came
down to breakfast; and the active mistress
herself had got through a good half day's
work. What a noisy, bustling pleasant place
was this Chilworth farmstead in comparison
with poor William Crisp's quiet house.
Through the open door of the kitchen you
caught a glimpse of the farm-yard, with cattle
feeding in the stalls, hens cackling to their
little broods, and ducks swimming in the
pond. The sunlight had a hard battle with
the roses and clematis, to force its way
through the latticed window through which
the soft fresh morning air swept in the scent
of the hayfields.

" Come and see our garden, Sarah dear,"
said her aunt, after the breakfast things had
been cleared away.

It was a treat to see such splendid guelder
roses, and stocks, and gilliflowers and sweet

peas, for Mrs. Fisher liked old fashioned flowers, declaring "they smelt the sweetest; and that those fine coloured things they got from foreign parts had nothing but their looks to recommend them."

"We shall get a famous crop of plums, this year, and that's a great blessing," said Mrs. Fisher, stopping at the orchard gate and leaning over it with her apron folded under her plump arms. "Robert is so very fond of plum pies and puddings."

"I hope you will not give the two lads the run of the orchard, aunt."

"No, indeed; I'll take care of that, Sarah. How pleasant it will be to bring our work in the summer evenings, into this bit arbour, and get Robert to read the Halifax paper to us. Do'st read poetry, lass?"

Sarah confessed she did not.

"Robert's very fond of poetry. He was reading a piece written by a tailor, living in Halifax, something about a dead child in its coffin."

The allusion to death made the tears course down poor Sarah's cheeks in an instant.

"Let me have my cry out, aunt," she said, as Mrs. Fisher put one arm round her waist and tried to soothe her in her kind, motherly way, "I shall be better for it afterwards."

"My dear child, I forgot your bereavements entirely," said Mrs. Fisher, the tears standing in her own eyes. "Oh! but death is a solemn thing for all of us to think about."

"And when death comes in a threefold way, as it did with ours," sobbed the poor girl, as she clung to the stout, kind-hearted being by her side, "it is indeed hard to bear. Thank God! they are spared further suffering."

The thought of her stern, yet tender-hearted father, being spared the misery of seeing the poor man's terrible enemy—want, enter his humble dwelling, did more to soothe Sarah's grief than anything else could.

"It would have been so fearful a trial to see him growing daily more haggard," she continued, "and heart-broken, as the well-preserved furniture disappeared piece-meal to supply the necessities of the family, and to know that death alone could bring the aid they all longed for. How mercifully God has dealt with both mother and father in taking them from the evil to come."

"We'll take the cart some fine day and go into Braidsworth, my love," said Mrs. Fisher, as she retraced her steps to the kitchen. "Robert shall drive us, if we can persuade him to leave his sketches for a day."

"I am told my cousin is very clever with his pencil," rejoined Sarah.

"Indeed he is. Mr. ——, the poet tailor, says he will be quite a genius that way one of these odd days. Your uncle had a view he took of the church framed and glazed, he thought so much of it, and Robert has a large scrap-book full of drawings. He is studying under some very clever artist from London, who is staying in Halifax just now. They say that kind of thing makes people ill-tempered, but it's not so with Robert, for a better tempered lad never existed."

Sarah said she was sure he was that, and then turned the conversation upon some other subject, for somehow she did not like Robert to form the topic of discussion, and she was glad when Tommy and Bobby came in, ravenously hungry and clamorous for dinner, for that gave Mrs. Fisher something to do.

CHAPTER VI.

It was really very provoking that Captain Vinen should receive Admiralty orders just at this juncture to rejoin his ship without delay, and sail at once to one of the West India stations, there was so much yet remaining to do, and William Gladstone had found such advantage from his cool headedness and decisive way of acting, that he felt he should get very badly on without him, now that his troubles were the thickest.

Captain Vinen had gone up to "The Rookery," the moment he had the news, with the Admiralty letter in his hand, and not finding Mr. Gladstone in the house had told his errand, with preface, to Frances, thus—

"I am going away to-morrow, Miss Frances. I have got my sailing orders for the West Indies."

He thought she changed colour at the announcement, and that her lips quivered as he spoke; but she rallied immediately.

"I am very sorry to hear it, Captain Vinen, for my brother's sake. Is it not rather a sudden recall?"

"It is; but just now, when everything is so unsettled, we must be prepared for that. When will William be home?"

"I expect him every minute. Has Amelia come back?"

"My mother has sent the carriage to bring her home to say 'good-bye' to me. I really am not worth so much trouble. Yet, as I shall probably be absent two or three years, I suppose she would not have been happy had she not seen the last of me."

"You will find great alterations in Braidsworth when you return."

"Yes, I suppose I shall have to come to

Bradford to see some of my old friends—if you are not all married."

"We shall scarcely all be that," rejoined Francis, smiling.

"I wish I could think so, Frances," said he, venturing to steal a glance into the pale expressive face that was turned upon him; "it would alleviate the pain of separation very much."

"Whatever happens, I can assure you, Captain Vinen, we shall always regard you with feelings of the liveliest gratitude," rejoined Frances, with apparent firmness.

He looked as if he wished to say something more, but his courage must have failed him just at the crisis, for after stammering some incoherent words, he all at once became silent, in which mood he remained until Mr. Gladstone entered the room.

"I regret to tell you that this is my farewell visit, Gladstone," he said, grasping his friend's hand; "I join my ship to-morrow."

"I am sorry to hear it, for my own sake,

but glad for yours, Alfred. 'The Invincible' is a very fine frigate, I believe."

" A perfect beauty. Could you not take a run down with me to Plymouth to see her ?"

" I really cannot ; that poor lad Jobson has to be brought before the magistrates to-morrow again, and I cannot possibly be absent. The case looks very black against him."

" I am sorry to hear that ; he must have had accomplices, one would think."

" He had not, for I am morally convinced he had nothing whatever to do with the fire," said William, decisively. " I would stake my life on that ; and yet, if nothing turns up to clear him to-morrow, he will certainly he committed for trial. His mother called on me to-day ; she is quite broken-hearted at the disgrace that has fallen upon her son."

" It is a very hard case; does the lad himself deny it ?"

" Not at all, and that goes more against him than anything else ; for the dogged silence

he maintains is enough to make anyone suspect him."

"I wish I had been staying over to-
morrow," said Captain Vinen, eagerly. "I
think I could have cleared the lad."

Gladstone shook his head, and looked in-
credulous as he said—

"I suppose it would be nonsense to ask
you to stay?"

"I should be court-martialled if I did," rejoined the Captain, with a laugh. "Well! it
is no use keeping myself on the rack in this
way. Go with me to the Rectory, William—
Miss Frances, I must bid you good-bye."

"Good-bye, Captain Vinen, I hope you will
not run any unnecessary risks, and that we
shall soon see you back again," said Frances.

"I cannot promise that. Good-bye and
God bless you!" and he took both her hands
in his, held them thus for a minute or more,
and then with a parting pressure let them
drop and was gone.

He came back the next minute, under pretence of having left his gloves, which were lying on the floor, and hoping to find Frances in tears at the very least. He found her sitting in the chair he had lately vacated, looking sad, but composed.

" Mind you don't go and work yourself to death in that school-room," he said, affecting a tone of severity as she picked up the gloves and gave them to him; " if you do, I for one will never forgive you."

" Do not be alarmed," was the answer. " I feel assured I shall never kill myself by hard work."

" Many get the same delusion into their heads when they commence, and only find out their mistake when it is too late. Such a fate should not be yours."

" Nor shall it. When you return I trust you will find me as healthy as I am now; if it should be otherwise, God will have ordained my trial for some all-wise purpose of His own."

She looked at him calmly and hopefully as she said this, for she felt bold in the strength of her own firm resolution.

" I see nothing can change you from your purpose," he said, twisting his gloves into all possible shapes as he stood facing her. " I believe love itself would fail before that stoical sense of duty you entertain."

A sudden light flashed through Frances's grey eyes, as she said—

" My duty is with my brother."

" Well, good-bye again," he added, abruptly, as he heard William calling to him from the garden. " God bless you !" and then he was fairly gone.

It was pleasant in after times to think how kindly he had parted from her, when everything connected with William's friend had become hallowed, as it were, by his own frank and generous nature. His " God bless you !" lingered with her when memory had almost forgotten the plain yet manly lineaments of

his face, and his short and hurried visit to
Braidsworth had almost passed into a tradi-
tion.

Frances rarely indulged in those dangerous
day-dreams, which weaken and degenerate the
character of so many young people now-a-
days, but sitting with her work in her lap,
after he had gone, she could scarcely fail to
draw a comparison between William Wilding
and Captain Vinen.

She was somewhat startled at the moment
when William Wilding's handsome, laughing,
face rose up in juxta-position to that of Alfred
Vinen, which was assuredly very much plainer.
The former charmed you at the first moment,
for no one could withstand the laughing light
that flashed from his eyes any more than they
could deny a manly beauty to his well-built,
athletic figure. When you looked again,
however, you felt there was something want-
ing. He was too handsome, too pleasant
looking to attract after the eye had become used to his fine face and figure. You

wanted strong, bold lines in that face to show you there was character within him. You wanted the eye to have a deeper light and the mouth a few more thoughtful curves than it possessed; you rarely saw Wilding's face without a smile upon it, for he was really a happy tempered being, and seldom permitted anything to disturb his philosophy, and this was the strongest proof that he was rarely in the habit of thinking profoundly.

Alfred Vinen, on the other hand, was very plain; but then you soon forgot this when you heard him fairly launched into a conversation he really liked; his usually cold, grey eye then lit up with excitement, his countenance became animated, and you discovered how expressive were those features, which looked dull and heavy when in repose. His voice betrayed the gentleman, if nothing else did, and added to his generous knowledge of human nature, and the extensive information his mind had treasured up during his sailing about the world, rendered him a peculiarly fascinating companion.

Frances' mind had already decided that she could never be satisfied with William Wilding; but she scarcely ventured to ask herself how far Alfred Vinen came up to her standard of a husband, for she had had, as yet, little encouragement to hope she was an object of interest to him; and now he would be absent for years, and who could tell what might happen to either or both of them in that interval.

She was very unhappy the rest of the day, notwithstanding all the philosophy she had called to her aid upon the subject, for she felt they had lost a staunch friend in Captain Vinen, whose place it would be very difficult to supply.

William told his sister that it had been a very painful parting at the Rectory, for Captain Vinen's honest, manly character, made him more than usually beloved, and that his father, in particular, had been painfully affected.

" We will go out to Longford as soon as I get done with this unpleasant business to-morrow," William said at night. " Poor Sophia, will think we have quite forgotten her."

" The funeral, you know, takes place the following day," was Frances's rejoinder.

" Poor Uncle Newman!   How suddenly he was taken off at last," said her brother, sadly. " I never should have thought such a thing as a fire would have killed him."

" Nor I, William."

" Staunton, the solicitor, gave me a hint to-day, when I met him, that he has left a very curious will," said William. " It was made several years since."

" If he had had time, perhaps he would have altered it," suggested Frances. " I am sure he would not have acted unjustly; it was only of late we thoroughly understood each other."

*   *   *   *

Uncle Newman's will was certainly as strange as Mr. Staunton had prepared William Gladstone to expect. After the plain and unostentatious funeral, the arrangements for which had been dictated in a paper written by the deceased, Mr. Staunton requested the attendance of the company in the dining-room to hear the reading of the document.

Mr. Banks was sitting near the table with his best ear—he was somewhat deaf in one of them—close to Mr. Staunton's chair. He had been a good deal connected with Mr. Newman in business matters, and rather expected he had been named an executor.

Mr. Staunton opened the will with that sharp, crackling sound, which all heirs expectant love to hear so well. Then he cleared his voice and read the long preamble with professional rapidity, until he came to the names of the executors, who proved to be Dr. Vinen and himself.

Mr. Banks uttered a low growl and

fidgetted in his chair. Mr. Staunton went on—

"To my dear niece Sophia Gladstone, I give and bequeath the sum of one thousand pounds lawful money, for her sole use and benefit."

"A cursed shabby legacy," muttered Mr. Banks, with a sarcastic smile.

"To my nieces, Kate Gladstone, and Frances Gladstone, a like sum of one thousand pounds for their sole use and benefit, to be held in trust for them, until they reach the respective ages of twenty-one, by my said executors."

"He's going to cut the lad off with a shilling," thought Mr. Banks, complacently.

"And to my nephew William Gladstone, I give and bequeath the sum of five thousand pounds, with my blessing. All the residue of my estate, lands, hereditaments, messuages, and tenements of whatever description, together with the sum of four thousand pounds which I am possessed of in the Three per Cent. Consols I give and bequeath to my executors, in trust for the purposes hereinafter named.

" I give and bequeath the sum of ten pounds yearly to ten poor married men, and ten poor married women of my native parish.

"I bequeath the sum of twenty pounds yearly to my faithful servant and friend, Jacob Friswell, in acknowledgment of his faithful services.

" All the residue of my estate I will and devise to my said executors for the sole use of my dear niece Sophia Gladstone, and direct that my said executors will dispose of my said house and lands at Longford, together with the household furniture, plate, linen, and books therein contained, to the best advantage, and pay over the proceeds, together with all the residue of my estate after the before mentioned legacies are discharged, on the fifth anniversary following my decease, to my said dear niece Sophia Gladstone."

"A cursed queer will that, Williamson," growled Mr. Banks, buttoning his coat and knitting his brows as he arose to leave the house, "and yet, by Jove, old Newman knew which way the cat would jump before long with that proud jackanapes of a nephew of his."

"He don't seem very much annoyed about it, either, Banks," said Mr. Williamson, a jovial, fox-hunting squire. "Five thousand pounds is a tolerable lump of money to fall in with."

"Pish, man, it will all be swallowed up in his fire," retorted Mr. Banks, striding out of the room as savagely as if he had been disappointed in a thumping legacy from old Newman himself. "He was in Tuesday's 'Gazette' at full length you know."

"Whew! that's a confounded deal worse than a black frost," cried Squire Williamson, taking his companion by the arm. "I'd recommend you, sir, to keep a sharp look out, if that's the case, with your high spirited filly at

'Sunnyside,' or he may take it into his head that her fat acres will replenish his coffers."

Mr. Banks laughed scornfully at such an idea.

"No! no, she's engaged to a man of my choosing, and other people need not try to fash their minds with the notion that a beggarly iron founder could run away with any one I have in hand," and thus speaking Mr. Banks departed.

"You must really take me home with you, William," was Sophia's first speech, when the brother told his sisters all the contents of uncle Newman's will. "I am so anxious for the sight of my own flowers and birds, that I could not rest another night at Longford."

William smiled to see how little importance she attached to her heiress-ship ; she had already forgotten it.

" The carriage can take us all home to-night, sister. We have no business here now that we have buried our dead out of our sight."

" Then let us go at once. Kate, run and

get my cloak and bonnet, whilst Frances pulls me one bunch of poor uncle Newman's Provence roses. I have those he brought me, only a very few short minutes before he was taken ill, in my work box."

" William," she continued, when both her sisters had left the room, "I wish from my heart our poor uncle had given you his property instead of me."

" I am very glad, Sophia, he did not. I scarcely know whether the handsome legacy he has left me will enable me to pay all my creditors."

" We have each a thousand pounds to add to it."

" I had rather die than take it, sister. I should be worse than a highwayman to rob you in that way."

" I shall never live to inherit my fortune," said Miss Gladstone, with a placid smile.

" Friswell has loaded the carriage with plants," said Frances, entering the room with an immense bunch of roses. "I am sure I cannot tell where we are to put them all in our little greenhouse."

"We shall find room for them, I am sure," said Sophia, cheerfully. "Poor Jacob will lose a good master, William."

"He will indeed. How sadly death breaks up a household. In another month, Longford will either own a new master, or we shall have an ugly, staring board confronting us on the lawn, whenever we come this way, with the announcement that the place is to let."

Kate at this moment came into the room with Sophia's bonnet and cloak, bringing the news that the servants had discovered Miss Gladstone was going home, and meditated a rather formidable leave taking.

Sophia disliked a scene above all things, especially at the present moment—when about to leave a place endeared to her by the remembrance of him who was now no more, and in which she had spent so many happy days.

" Be quick, Kate, and give me my cloak and bonnet, so that I may be ready to depart," Sophia said, with the hurried nervous manner she had when deeply affected. " Frances, don't leave the roses ; now, William, your arm, love," and clinging to her brother, she was carried rather than walked down the stairs.

It was too late. The women, with the gardener and Jacob Friswell, were already standing in the hall they had to pass through, one or two with their aprons up to their eyes, and all looking very grave and sad in their deep mourning.

" You must come to see me at Braidsworth," said Sophia, kindly, as she shook hands with each. " This parting is very painful to all of us."

" You should have stopped here, Miss Sophia," said Jacob, glumly.

" I am sorry, Friswell, I cannot. Now, good-bye, again."

Miss Gladstone suffered her brother to carry her to the carriage, seated in which, her fortitude forsook her, and she cried like a child nearly all the way to Braidsworth.

The sight of " The Rookery " somewhat revived her. Old Hannah was standing at the porch ready to welcome them home again, after her own fashion, and to her master's astonishment, decently dressed in black.

" I'm thankful to get ye all back again, hinnies," she said, as Frances alighted first. " I'll never part wi' ye again for so long, I'll warrant that. Oh! Miss Sophia, whatever have you brought those nasty bushes for, when we've more now than we know what to do with ?"

" We shall find room for them, Hannah," said Sophia.

" Faix! I'd soon do that, if I'd my own way wi' them," she continued, lifting Miss Gladstone out of the carriage with all the ease possible. " Oh! hinnies, but the black dress brings back past sorrows to one's mind! I've kept the tea back for a full hour for your coming."

" This is pleasant, indeed," said Miss Gladstone, looking around her pretty sitting-room,
with a cheerful smile. " I have spent so many
happy hours in this flowery prison of mine,
that I return to it with all the delight one
feels in greeting a long absent friend."

" We shall have to part with it very soon,
Sophia," said Frances, sadly.

" Let us enjoy it whilst we can, then,
Frances. We will make our next nest quite
as dear to us."

" Frances, you have allowed that piano to
get wretchedly out of tune," said Kate, running her fingers over the keys, which certainly
jangled somewhat.

" We have had more serious things to
think about, Kate. The fire is to blame for
all."

" That odious fire! I hope William will
get the villains well punished who did the
mischief," said Kate, wrathfully.

" As far as poor Harry Jobson is concerned,
you have your wish, Kate," rejoined her

younger sister. " William told me this morning the magistrates have committed him for trial, and sent him to York Castle."

Even Kate could not restrain an exclamation of pity at this announcement.

" How grieved I am for Sarah Crisp !" said Sophia.

"And so am I, Sophia," was Kate's observation. " Where is Sarah ?"

" At Chilworth, with some relatives. They buried poor William Crisp and his wife yesterday. Hannah said it was pitiable to see the two coffins laid both in one grave, close beside poor little Jessie."

" If Harry Jobson did set fire to the foundry," said Kate, after a pause, " all the deaths it has caused are enough to drive him mad. I would not have his reflections for the whole world."

" William says he is quite convinced he is innocent. But he was seen close to the premises within half-an-hour of the fire being discovered, and he will give no account of how he spent the interval between that time and his coming home, near midnight, which told very much against him."

" Well, I hope it will all be cleared up before long," added Miss Gladstone, anxiously. " I remember Harry as a fine and spirited lad, when Sarah and he used to come hand in hand up to 'The Rookery' with messages from William. Somehow I think with our brother that he cannot have done such a very serious crime as firing William's foundry."

CHAPTER VII.

Autumn came, and a busy one it was for the family at "The Rookery." Uncle Newman's legacy helped to pay the deficiency in Mr. Gladstone's assets, that the fire, &c., had caused, and left a trifling surplus even after that.

"The Rookery" was let to an excellent tenant, a gentleman of the name of Silvester, whose ladylike wife and handsome son would certainly make it quite as attractive to a certain set as their predecessors had done. They were to take possession immediately, if Mr. Gladstone could find a house in Bradford that would suit him, as Mrs. Silvester was quite tired of Bath, where they were then staying, and as Mr. Gladstone was to enter upon his new employment on the first of September, he was just as anxious to effect a removal.

Frances and her brother walked with weary hearts for this purpose through the pretty suburbs of Bradford, and more than once they were tempted to give up the pursuit in despair ; but at length they found a small but pleasant house in one of the terraces, where the rent was not very extravagant, and which could boast a view quite as diversified as that Sophia had from her window at " The Rookery." This they hired.

" It's great recommendation to me," said Frances, as she reclined in an easy chair— at night, after the house had been really taken, and the landlord had given up the key to her brother—with the luxurious feeling of ex- haustion which a really bustling day incites us to indulge, " lies in its having an outlet at the back, which takes you into some real country fields. I thought of you, Sophia, dear, when the landlord pointed this out, and the look I gave William at the moment decided him."

" I hope we shall have pleasant neighbours," said Kate.

" I can tell you the names on each side, at any rate," said Frances, cheerfully. " Mr. and Mrs. Jeremy live on the right, and as I caught a glimpse of a very tastefully laid out garden, I hope they will come up to your standard, Kate. William knows Mr. Jeremy, but he was so busy talking to the landlord about alterations and repairs that I could not learn who he was. They call the people on the other side Ryan, I believe."

" The name is enough !" said Kate, satirically.

" Don't say that until you see them, Kate. There is a charming room facing the south-west, Sophia, which William and I have already determined shall be devoted to you. It is quite as large as this, and William says he can get the self-same paper for the walls, to deceive you into the delusion you are still at 'The Rookery.' The bay window will make a charming conservatory, if properly managed."

" And the school-room, Frances ?"

" Will not disturb you in the least; it's quite at the other end of the house. It has a French window opening upon a grass plot, which is a great advantage. William tried to persuade me to give up the idea of a school; but it was useless, for I am resolved to carry it out. I did not tell him we intended laying by uncle Newman's legacy to start him in business again; but I suspect he fancies some idea of the kind."

" When do we remove, Frances ?" asked Kate.

" Next week; the house is in such capital repair that it requires very little to be done to it. A little papering and painting, and a new kitchen-range, the present being very much the worse for wear. These trifles, with the mending a few panes of glass, I believe, comprise all the requirements. I shall remove your goods and chattels, Sophia, bushes, as Hannah calls them, and all."

Nothing could be pleasanter than her whole manner, as she talked on in her eager, cheerful way, putting fresh heart into her hearers, both of whom were too much accustomed to depend upon her, whenever a difficulty arose. She really looked lovely, with her sparkling eyes and clear complexion as she lay back in her chair, with an affectation of idleness that was far from her thoughts. Could Captain Vinen have seen her at that moment it would have made him forget the discomforts of his voyage a little.

That week was truly an uncomfortable period for all; but it was passed through, and the Sabbath morn came in bright and beautiful once more, on quiet Braidsworth. Frances's unfailing energy and her good temper had carried them on triumphantly through all the trouble, but it sent a chill even through her

brave heart, when, on coming down to breakfast, she saw the hall filled with covered-up
furniture, and caught a glimpse in passing of
the bare dismantled rooms.

"I am glad our last Sunday at Braidsworth is so bright and balmy," she said, as
she sat at the head of the table. "We shall
take away with us to Bradford nothing but
the remembrance of sunshiny beauty, connected with our early home."

"I always think a fine Sunday calmer and
brighter than any week-day," said Sophia,
thoughtfully.

"I suppose there is less smoke and noise,
Sophia," remarked her brother.

"Yes, and people go about more quietly
and leisurely on the Sabbath. Does it not
make you all sad," she continued, "to think
that this is our last of many happy Sundays
at Braidsworth?"

"We shall come back again," said Frances,
hopefully and confidently.

"I trust so. I should, indeed, be unhappy

if I thought it was a final parting," observed Sophia, eagerly. " We have all been so very, very happy here !"

They had indeed, and Sophia not the least so, notwithstanding her sad misfortune.

" Only wait until you see our new house," said Frances, gaily, "it is really pretty enough to prevent our fretting for ' The Rookery.' I had no idea of seeing such beautiful scenery near a large town."

" Frances never desponds," said Kate, who had been pursuing her own thoughts. " I remember when she was a little girl, she used to say she would work for her own living."

" I hope I shall like it, Kate. Come, there is the first bell," said Frances.

They were all surprised to see Sophia get up with the rest, and say she was going to church.

" I must go this last time," she said.

Frances understood and respected the feeling that prompted her to undergo so much fatigue ; but it was not without many misgiv-

ings she dressed her in her black silk cloak
and bonnet, lest her strength should give way
before the service was over.

"I feel very much stronger to-day, Frances,"
she said, with her quiet smile, " so you must
not be alarmed for me, my love."

"'I am not alarmed, Sophia."

" Why do your hands tremble so, then ?"
she asked.

" The hard work they have gone through
during the week, I suppose makes them do
so.   There, I have tied your bonnet, notwithstanding.   I really think we must be extravagant enough to persuade our brother to
keep the pony-chaise ; it will be so pleasant to
drive over here sometimes."

" I thought we were to be so economical,
Frances ?"

" So we will.   That true economy, which
is quite as far removed from parsimony
as extravagance.   Yes, William must really
keep the old pony and the chaise.   Can you
walk down stairs, Sophia ?"

Miss Gladstone was soon comfortably seated beside her brother, and Kate and Frances set off to walk to church. The road was beautiful enough to make it a matter of choice to do so in most weathers, and on this particular morning every object seemed particularly lovely, when seen under that cloudless sky.

"How calm and bright everything appears," said Kate, as they came within sight of the church.

"It does indeed," returned Frances. "I like to see the Braidsworth people, coming from all quarters, dressed in their Sunday best. Look, Kate, there is Dr. Vinen's broad brimmed hat just passing beneath the vestry door."

"Who is that talking to Sophia?" cried Kate, who had been watching the pony chaise for the last minute.

"Miss Coulson, I think. At any rate that is her livery servant holding the horses just behind. She surely cannot have ridden from 'Sunnyside' this morning."

It was Miss Coulson who was helping poor
Sophia to alight, and it was Miss Coulson's
arm that she was leaning upon, as they
advanced with William to meet the two
girls.

It was into her brother's face that Frances
looked, rather than into that one fresher and
brighter she had immediately before her,
placed on a line with the pale, sad face of her
own sister. The expression she saw in it
puzzled her so much that she turned at length
to Agatha herself.

" I heard Dr. Vinen was to preach a charity
sermon this morning, my dear," said Agatha,
shaking hands with both Frances and Kate,
" and this, added to my anxiety to see you
once again at Braidsworth before you left,
tempted me to ride over and inflict my company on you for the day."

" Would not Mrs. Coulson come as well ?"
one of them asked.

" Mr. Briscoe returned last night, and Dr.
Vinen and he are not sufficiently good friends

for him to ride so far to hear one of your good rector's sermons."

During this conversation, the four girls (if we may be permitted to include Sophia with the rest) were walking up the churchyard, exchanging a kindly greeting with several people in their progress, and, as the bell ceased, they entered the sacred edifice.

Frances's dread lest Sophia's strength should fail her, was dissipated when she noticed the devotional calmness of her manner. The sermon, fortunately, was not a long one, and the congregation were departing before the usual time, notwithstanding the collection which Agatha Coulson had prepared them to expect.

Dr. Vinen joined them at the porch.

"I honour the feeling, Sophia, that brings you here to-day," he said, offering her his arm.

"I am very glad I came, Dr. Vinen. I thought I was a small child again, when I listened to your sermon," she said.

" Yet it was quite a new one, my dear. I suppose you leave us to-morrow ?"

" We do, sir; Frances has issued the command to march, and such poor useless things as William and I must be content to obey her. I believe our Bradford house is very pleasantly situated."

" I was there yesterday," said her companion, " and can verify Frances's report on that point."

" Come to the Rectory and dine with us," he said, as William drew up at the end of the lane. " I have news from Alfred to tell you."

None of them, however, seemed disposed to accept his invitation. Even Miss Coulson declined it, heartily as it was given.

" This last day," said Sophia, " must be spent at home."

" I expect Mr. Briscoe over to take my duty this afternoon," said the rector, addressing himself particularly to Miss Coulson. " Did he say anything about it before you left ?"

" Not a word. In fact, he was still in bed," she said, with a curl of her lip.

" Some one must teach him better manners when he gets married," said the jovial Rector, shaking hands all round. " I hope he will come, because it will enable me, after service, to bring him up to ' The Rookery.' "

Agatha evidently did not relish the prospect of her lover's company at all, and reiterated her conviction that Dr. Vinen would have to do the duty himself. The event proved she was correct, for Mrs. Coulson's dinner was particularly good, and Mr. Briscoe ate heartily. That and the port wine made him drowsy, and he fell asleep.

" What do you think of Mr. Briscoe?" Agatha asked Kate, as they sauntered slowly on their way to ' The Rookery.' " I think he is handsome."

" He is generally reckoned so, and I sup-pose he is," she answered, in a tone of great indifference. " He has a good figure and gen-

tlemanly manners to the world at large—
consequently the world speaks him fair." ·

"Is he a pleasant man, Agatha?" asked
her companion, thinking of William Wilding.

"No!" said Miss Coulson, with strange
bitterness; "yet the world believes him to
be such, for there is a suavity in his bear-
ing that makes you forget, sometimes, the
utter want of heart the animal conceals beneath those polished manners and that cold
smiling face. How I detest those good looking, callous-souled beings one continually
meets with," she added, with unwonted
bitterness.

" Do you judge only from Mr. Briscoe,
Agatha," asked Kate.

"I do not! I have met many, Kate.
There was a gentleman at Scarborough last
year when we were there, whom half the
women went wild about, the silly fools. I could
not bear him for his icy selfishness and self-
laudation, and shunned his society. I heard,

a month ago, one sweet girl whose affections he had won had just died broken-hearted at his desertion, caused by the loss of her fortune."

" The paltry villain !"

" The base scoundrel ! Yet, Kate, I would wager any money some other silly moth has already been caught by the glare and tinsel of his handsome face, and the flattery of his false tongue. It makes one savage to think of a lover being handsome."

" I'm sure I should not like to marry an ugly man," said Kate, who was completely carried out of her depth by her companion's vehemence.

" Nor I, Kate; and yet I would rather marry a plain man who had a heart and a mind than a handsome fool without either. There is nothing very terrible in an ugly face, after all, when one gets accustomed to it."

" But it would take a very long time to do that," said Kate. " Why should handsome men be disagreeable ?"

"For no reason whatever that I know, except, perhaps, that Nature — who is much more just than her children—gives affection to one to whom she has played the niggard in outward appearance."

"I would not marry Mr. Briscoe, then, Agatha."

"What would you do?" asked Miss Coulson, quickening her pace as Frances looked back.

"I would run away; or, as 'Sunnyside' is your property and not his, I'd order him off the premises, and if he wouldn't go, I'd desire my groom to turn him out."

"Capital advice, Kate! I will order Mr. Briscoe to shoulder his knapsack the moment I get home," said Agatha, laughing. "There is Frances looking back again."

*   *   *   *   *   *

William Wilding was sitting in the porch waiting for them, having walked over to spend the day with Mr. Gladstone. Agatha watched

Kate's beautiful face, mantling with blushes, as she stood talking to him in a low tone, after all the rest had shaken hands with him; and she was compelled to confess that beauty of person and warmth of heart might go together as they did in the person of Kate's lover.

He was not as striking looking as Mr. Briscoe, but still he was handsome, and Kate was evidently happy. She took him by the arm, and led him into the garden. They were visiting their favourite haunts together for the last time.

The afternoon passed over more rapidly than any of them anticipated. It was six o'clock, and Agatha arose to depart, Mr. Gladstone insisting upon accompanying her home.

" I have my servant," she said, though hoping he would persist in his determination.

" I should not be easy, even with his protection, if I did not see you safe at home," he replied.

"I will make an errand into Bradford very soon, girls," she cried, as they stood at 'The Rookery' gates. "Now, Mr. Gladstone, I am quite ready."

They rode off.

"I am sorry to take you so far to-night," she said, when they were some distance on the road. "You will have to ride six miles alone."

"That's not disagreeable," said her companion, "on a fine night at the end of September."

"Well, I'm glad you don't mind the ride."

His spirits rose with the excitement of her conversation addressed entirely to himself, and knowing that every look and every word, for the next hour at any rate, would be entirely his own. Agatha, too, seemed to forget that 'Sunnyside' and the Rev. Mr. Briscoe would have to be encountered ere long.

"This is very pleasant, indeed," she said, pulling up her pony on the brow of a hill to admire the scenery, lit up by a cloudless moon. " That ivy-covered ruin would make a capital ' bit' for a painter. See! how prettily you catch the reflection of the light in the water."

" These autumn nights are, indeed, beautiful," responded William, with the tone of one who wished to prolong a conversation for the sake of listening to his companion's voice.

" Yes. And yet we enjoy them with a something approaching trouble, mixed with the pleasure we never experience either in spring or summer, because we know they will soon give way to dreary winter. The first withered leaf I find in my walks always makes me sad."

" Is not that an unhealthy feeling, Miss Agatha ?" said her companion.

" Perhaps so."

" Winter," continued Mr. Gladstone, " has beauties of its own, which a rightly constituted mind can enjoy just as keenly as the richer glories of autumn. Imagine this to be a winter night, keen, dry, starry, and picture yourself riding from Braidsworth to 'Sunny-side' with the recollection of the bright, warm room, and the many voices you have left still ringing in your ears."

"I admit the beauty of the picture," said Agatha in a subdued tone.

" Then remember the warm 'Sunnyside' parlour lighted only by a blazing fire, with the pictures half in light and half in shade hanging upon the walls."

" And Mr. Briscoe's cold, handsome face darkening the picture," thought Miss Coulson.

William wondered she did not reply.

" I am afraid," said he softly, " you do not think me a very accurate sketcher, Miss Agatha."

" I see it all," she said, with a quiet bitter-ness in her voice, that somehow made his heart leap wildly, as he watched her drooping figure, " when we are happy, quietly happy, your picture would be enjoyable."

Agatha felt the tears flowing from her eyes as she spoke, although her voice did not falter, and knowing how dangerous it was to give way to such thoughts, she changed the conversation, saying—

" Frances's hopefulness does me good to witness. I scarcely thought any one who owned a woman's heart could display so much heroism of the most valuable kind."

" She shames us all," said her brother, with a glowing cheek. " Even I must confess to a cowardly shame at the idea of her keeping a school."

" I admire her for it. I wish her example was more generally followed by the wives and daughters of the present day. There would be fewer old maids wasting out a sluggish existence, I am certain. Take my word for it, your own sex will admire your sister the more for this undertaking. I am sure it won't decrease her chance of getting a good husband."

" I am very glad to hear one of her own sex applauding her conduct. It is, however, a wearisome employment for an active, ardent mind."

" Not in the least. Duty will hallow her efforts. I am sure Frances is very happy in the idea."

" Yes, but she has not yet experienced the petty annoyances of drumming learning into twenty or thirty stupid girls."

" Are any girls stupid, Mr. Gladstone ? I have met with stupid boys, and stupid men in plenty, but I never yet met with a girl who was naturally stupid. I always find some error of rearing and education to be at the root of the evil in them. Just watch a roomful of romping, happy girls, when their spirits have had time to expand beneath the influence of companionship, and tell me, if you can see one dark or stupid face amongst them."

Her companion was forced to confess he could not at the moment name a stupid girl within the range of his acquaintances; but then he knew so few ; young men in business had little opportunity of observing the female character.

" Frances has nothing to fear," continued Miss Coulson, " I have half a mind to take office under her myself."

" We had better start a female college at once," said William, rather sarcastically. " Who is this riding towards us I wonder ?"

" Mr. Briscoe, perhaps ; what an achievement to have ridden half a mile from the ' Sunnyside' gates, in search of the strayed sheep," said Miss Coulson, contemptuously.

" There is not much love there," thought William, as the new comer, who proved to be Mr. Briscoe, stopped and spoke.

" Your mother is rather uneasy, Agatha, I can assure you," he said, in his cold proud tones. " Do you know it is nearly ten o'clock ?' "

" I do, Mr. Briscoe. Allow me to introduce Mr. Gladstone, who has kindly volunteered to guard me against all the dangers of a September ride from Braidsworth to 'Sunny-side.'"

Mr. Briscoe was armour proof against the haughty manner his mistress assumed towards him. She knew that he was, and yet she always bore herself proudly perhaps, with the faint hope that there might some day be found an unguarded place in his mail of pride, through which a contemptuous shaft might be sent.

"I hope your sleep after dinner did you good," she said, as he turned his horse's head round. "Dr. Vinen, I believe, expected you to take his afternoon duty."

"I could not come, Mrs. Coulson would not part with me," he said coldly.

"I wish she would marry him," thought Agatha, angrily. "Did you go to church, sir, this afternoon ?" she asked.

"No, I had a head-ache."

"The effect of eating and drinking at dinner," thought Agatha.

" The ' Sunnyside' curate is thought a very good preacher," observed Mr. Gladstone.

" Pretty well," rejoined Mr. Briscoe, rather scornfully. " Rather feeble, I take it."

" Oh! he's only a curate," retorted Agatha. "How eloquent he would become if he were made rector. Mr. William, ride up to the house and take the brunt of mamma's lecture on yourself, Mr. Briscoe never screens me when I am in fault," continued Agatha, as they entered the grounds.

Mr. Gladstone assented, and on gaining the door assisted her to alight. Mrs. Coulson was fidgetty and anxious, and rather cross, but William's quiet manner soon soothed her.

" My love! Mr. Briscoe has spent the whole day by himself. Not a creature has called," she said pathetically.

" I am sorry for it," said Miss Coulson, taking a candlestick from the sideboard. " Good night, Mr. Gladstone," and she held out her hand. " The night air has made me very drowsy."

"But Mr. Briscoe, Agatha!" said her mother, quite shocked at such rudeness.

"Good-night, Mr. Briscoe," she said, dropping a haughty curtsey, as she swept out of the room.

CHAPTER VIII.

" I CANNOT think, Charles," said Mrs. Fisher, as she sat, with her work in her lap, beside her husband one evening as he smoked his pipe in that comfortable kitchen, " for the life of me, Charles, I cannot think what our Sarah pines so about. It's well into three weeks since she came, and yet she's still the same poor white thing she was at first, with an arm no thicker than my thumb!" No mean thickness either was this said thumb. "And I'm sure it cannot be for them that are dead and gone she cries and frets so sadly."

" I'm sure, Helen, I cannot tell what ails her," said Farmer Fisher, knocking the ashes

out of his pipe as he spoke. "Hast thee
asked her what she frets for?"

"I have, Charles."

"Well, what does she say?"

"Nothing to speak of. She says it's the
weather."

"It's beautiful fine weather, wife. Does
Sarah not like it?"

"Oh! it's not the weather," continued Mrs.
Fisher, knitting very fast, and looking both
angry and perplexed. "I'm afraid, Charles,
that our Sarah is in love!"

"In love! the deuce!"

"Yes, in love, Charles. I'll have Robert
asked this very night."

"But thee doesn't think, Helen, that the
lass is in love wi' our Robert?" demanded
her husband, looking very keenly at his wife.
"She's no match for him, I'm thinking."

"No, no, it's not our Robert at all. It's
somebody at Braidsworth. What else could
make her fret and fume as she does?"

"Well, Helen, if it's not Bob, it's no great

matter of ourn," rejoined her husband, resuming his pipe. "Take my advice, and don't meddle or make with what's no business of yours; if Sarah Crisp has a sweetheart, what's that to you, I'd like to know?"

"Not much, certainly, Charles, but still it's something. I shouldn't like her to throw herself away on any bad, ne'er-do-well. I wish thou'd ask Henry Salmon the next time thou'rt in Braidsworth."

"I'll do nothing of the kind. That's playing spy, Helen."

"Well, husband, thou know'st best. Sarah is thy niece."

"And a very modest, decent lass she is into the bargain," said the uncle, proudly. "I'll never disown my own flesh and blood, wife."

"I don't wish that you should, Charles," said his wife. "I am only anxious the dear girl shouldn't form a connexion that might make her miserable for life."

The subject of this conversation was at the moment sitting on the edge of a coppice about half a mile from the farm. A thunder storm the preceding summer had shattered a magnificent oak in such a manner that little more than the stump was left, and this stump, jagged and torn as it was into a dozen fantastic shapes, made a very pleasant seat for two or three people.

Sarah was the only occupant, for Bobby and Tommy were scrambling about the wood in search of nuts, whilst Robert had thrown himself along a rock that had been shattered by the same storm which had devastated the oak, and was watching with a kind of lazy interest the varying tints of the evening sky, as he saw them reflected in a piece of water before him.

The scene itself was charming. The place where they were sitting was the centre of a sort of rustic amphitheatre formed by the wood which surrounded it, whilst at their feet a small clear sheet of water lay calm as a mirror reflecting the setting sun.

Robert looked at the lake, and then at his

cousin, who was pale and pensive, apparently more busy with her own thoughts than with the beauteous scene around her. He turned to the lake again, saying somewhat abruptly—

"Would you like to live in Bradford, Sarah ?"

"In Bradford, Robert !" was her answer, as she started and looked at him in some surprise. "Why do you ask me ?"

"I don't exactly know," he rejoined, eyeing her furtively, although he affected to be trying to catch a branch that hung over his head. "I thought you liked Bradford, perhaps."

"I have never been there more than three or four times. Father didn't like me to go."

"Then you don't know anyone there, I suppose ?" he asked.

"Oh, yes. There's Miss Thorne and cousin Simpkins."

"Who is Miss Thorne, Sarah ?" interrupted Robert.

"A dressmaker."

"The dressmaker Fanny was with ?"

Sarah nodded.

"Well, I don't think she's any great shakes. And who's this cousin Simpkins."

"An ironfounder."

"A master ironfounder?"

"Yes, and a very rich one. Father often talked of going to call upon him," said Sarah.

"And why didn't he?"

"Why? I fancy it was because he was so very rich, Robert. Father, you know, was very proud; too proud, perhaps, for a poor man, and couldn't bear to court rich folks, like cousin Simpkins."

"So he never went, I suppose?"

"Never."

"Well, then, we'll go the next time we are in Bradford, cousin. I hope this cousin Simpkins is not proud."

"Not in the least, Robert. I remember his coming over to Braidsworth to see father, and he wasn't in the least proud then, and I should think he isn't changed, for somehow one couldn't imagine that a man with such a hearty voice and pleasant face could alter in that way. I remember father saying he didn't like to go near them because of Mrs. Simpkins."

" What's the matter with her, Sarah?" asked Robert.

" Why, you know, cousin, we shouldn't judge people by hearsay; but father had heard she was rather a selfish kind of woman, and not over fond of her husband's friends, and this kept him away, or, from going as he would have done."

" We'll go for all that, Sarah. Suppose we return to the farm now," and he sat up and yawned.

Sarah was in no hurry to move. She liked her pleasant mossy seat, and the view it commanded of wood and water, and she liked to hear Robert talk in that brotherly way to her. Her companion, however, would sit no longer. He wanted to be at home for some particular reason of his own, and he began to halloa to Tommy and Bobby, who were almost out of hearing, judging by the faint answers they re- turned.

The pleasant twilight began to darken around them by the time they were clear of the wood and fairly on their way homewards.

"Here's a letter for you, Sarah," said her aunt, as they entered the kitchen, holding out a square, badly-folded, ill-directed letter. "I suppose it's from Mr. Salmon, or somebody at Braidsworth, judging from the post-mark."

"Uncle Henry can write better than that, aunt," said Bobby, peeping over his sister's shoulder, as she held the letter in her hand, with a bewildered look.

"Never mind who it's from, Bobby," said Robert, coming to Sarah's aid, as he saw how the colour came and went on her cheek. "Run into the garden and see if I left my easel stick there this morning."

"I saw it in the summer house," said Tommy, jumping up and making for the door. "Ah! cousin Robert, hold Bobby back till I get it for you."

In the scuffle that followed between the three Sarah stole away to her own little room with the letter in her bosom.

She had to strike a light before she could read it, for it had become quite dark. It was a long time ere that light could be obtained, her hand trembled so with the anxious terror that filled her heart, but having succeeded she locked the door gently and seated herself to read the precious letter.

She knew Henry Jobson's sprawling, mis-shapen writing in a moment. Eager as she was to learn what Henry had to say, she sat turning the missive over and over without opening it for several minutes, scanning the direction—" Miss Crisp, Mr. Charles Fisher's, Chilworth," till she had every down stroke off by heart; and wondering how it came to be so dirty, as if it had been carried in some-body's pocket, and thinking that Harry must certainly be at liberty, or it would have had the York post-mark on it instead of the Braidsworth.

At last she took courage and opened it.

Harry was no scholar, but there was a rough kind of passion breathing through his homely, ill-written letter, that made Sarah's heart beat wildly, as she deciphered, with some difficulty, the following lines :—

" York Castle, Sept. 20, 18—

" Dearest Sarah,

" I have been in jail a fortnight or more, and suppose I shall have to lie here another month or more before I am put on my trial. I've lost all count of time, somehow, for one day drags on after another in this sickening dungeon, with no one but my poor old mother and a comrade or two that won't think me guilty of the horrid crime I'm charged with, comes near me at all. Dear Sarah, I did think you would come first of all to cheer a poor fellow a bit, but suppose you've had to meet so much trouble of your own that you've no pity to spare for others. Dear Sarah, mother told me all about the grief you've been in, and God knows how bitterly I cried for you when I couldn't cry for myself. Don't think badly of me for that, but believe me when I tell you I love you with all my heart and soul. I could slay myself sometimes, I lose heart so, and then I rally again when I think they never can find a poor fellow guilty just because he was near that unlucky foundry an hour or so before it burst into a blaze.

"Mr. Gladstone has been here, and sorely grieved he looked to see me dressed up in the filthy jail dress they put on me here. They shouldn't dress folks who are innocent in the eye of the law, as Henry Salmon says, like thieves and murderers. He says he is sure I'm not guilty, but what good will that do when I dare not point out them that is? Mother is going to put this letter into the Braidsworth post for me, so I must conclude.

"If you love me, Sarah, come and see me. Don't be ashamed or afraid, for there's many an honest man breaking his heart in jail, and

many a villain walking about at large. God
bless you.

"Yours till death,

"HARRY JOBSON."

"P.S.—You must get a magistrate's order
before you come, or they won't let you in."

*   *   *   *

It took Sarah a full hour to decipher Harry's
meaning. She cried so bitterly over his
simple letter, and the writing in many places
being so indifferent it was very difficult to
comprehend the whole until she had read
it a second time. Then her candle went out
and she had to sit in the dark, thinking over
what he had written, and trying to decide
upon what she should do.

York was very far off, but if she could get
to Bradford there was a coach that would
take her there in something less than a day;
then there was the justice's order to obtain,
and that would probably delay her in Braidsworth three or four hours, if not more. She

determined to ask Robert to drive her to Bradford, and they could call at Braidsworth in passing; and drying her tears she went downstairs with a strengthened heart.

Robert was sitting alone in the kitchen, sketching a head in crayons by the light of a guttering candle.

" Snuff the candle, Sarah, if you please," said he in his calm, quiet manner, without looking round, for he knew it must be her light step on the sanded floor.

Sarah snuffed the candle, and stood leaning over his chair. Robert pursued his occupation in silence for eight or ten minutes, during which time the head was sketched, and he began to shade it.

" You are very silent, Sarah," he said, at length looking up into her pale face. " Why, Sarah, you have been crying," he added, as he noticed how red her eyes were. " May I ask what has happened ?"

Sarah could only reply by placing the letter in his hands, asking him to read it.

Robert took a long time to read the missive,

but he got to the end at last. No one could have dreamt that he loved his cousin, almost as passionately as Harry Jobson did, from the cool, methodical way in which he folded and returned it to her. Sarah herself never suspected this, or she would not have given one lover the letter of another to read.

"When do you intend to go, Sarah?" he asked, for he never dreamed, with that wretched face, blistered with tears, and those red eyes, she could do anything else.

"To-morrow, Robert, if I can be spared. You see poor Harry is very miserable, and I could not stay here longer without seeing him," said Sarah, drying her tears. "If you would drive me to Bradford I could easily manage the rest."

"I'll do that, my poor girl."

"And, Robert, if you would tell uncle and aunt about Harry, and assure them, too, we are certain he is innocent, and that it will all come out at the trial, I should be very thankful to you."

"I'll do all that, Sarah dear. I'll tell

mother first, and leave it to her to break it to father when they go to bed. He won't make any objection, I'm sure, to your going to Bradford, for he could not resist that pale, pleading face.

"Thank you, dear Robert," said Sarah, tremblingly.

"Mother knows a decent woman that lives in some part of York, that you could go and stay with," said Robert, after a moment's consideration. "She lives a great distance from the Castle, but you will be quite safe with her, and very comfortable as well. I'll ask mother for her address in the morning before we start."

"Thank you, cousin."

"When does the trial come on, Sarah?" asked Robert.

"Not for two months or more, I believe, cousin. Two long, weary months," said the poor girl, sighing.

"It's a fearfully long time to be in prison, Sarah; but it will pass away somehow.

I think you had better go to bed and
get a good night's rest if you can. I
will tell your aunt all when she comes in, and
we will start after breakfast to-morrow.
Good-night."

And Robert shook her warmly by the hand.

Sarah little dreamed, as she dragged her
weary limbs upstairs to bed, what a sad,
heavy heart she was leaving behind her with
poor Robert. It was, indeed, a bitter trial to
aid the girl, he secretly loved, to comfort his
rival with her presence ; but he resolved from
the first to do what he bravely thought lay
within the line of his duty, and though the
struggle was both long and severe, he con-
quered at last, and tried to be content to see
another preferred before himself.

When Mrs. Fisher came in with all the
eager bustle that characterised her, Robert
put the sketch he had been engaged upon
aside, and called his mother to him.

"What is it you want, Robert?" she asked,
looking into his face.

" Sit down, mother, and I'll tell you," he rejoined, placing a chair close to his own.

" Don't you see I'm very busy, my lad," she said, still bustling and fussing about the kitchen.

" Sit down a minute, mother, and listen to me," said Robert, getting up, and putting his arm round her waist to keep her where she was. " I want to tell you something."

" Be quick then."

" I'll be as quick as I can, mother, although I am afraid I shall scarcely be able to make you understand everything I have to relate all at once."

" Then why don't you begin ?"

" Well, Sarah wants to go to York."

" Then she sha'n't go, Robert," said Mrs. Fisher, perversely. " I won't hear of a young girl like Sarah going such a distance all by herself."

" But, mother, Sarah must go," said her son, calmly.

" And what for, pray?" demanded Mrs.

Fisher, putting on one of her severest looks. "There's nobody in York she can want to see, I'm quite confident."

"There is, mother."

"Son, have done with you," as Robert's arm pressed her ample waist somewhat tightly. "I'm sure I never heard of any human being the Crisps knew in York."

"It is no one who lives in York Sarah wants to see; it's only within the last few days that he has gone there. Sarah has a sweetheart, mother, who is accused of setting fire to Mr. Gladstone's foundry, and he has been committed to York Castle within the last few days."

"Sarah Crisp's sweetheart in York Castle, Robert?" cried Mrs. Fisher, in no small astonishment; "it is not possible."

"It is not only possible but quite true; and what's more, mother, Sarah must go and see him at once," said her son.

Robert ruled his mother with that quiet speaking ten times more than he ever could have accomplished by all the blustering and hectoring in the world. It was a very rare thing for her to resist so long in complying with his behests as was the case in the present instance, but then this affair of Sarah was something so peculiarly strange.

" What will your father say, Robert, when he hears the news ?" asked Mrs. Fisher, after a pause.

" You must tell my father to-night, mother," said her son, quietly; " he won't say much, as it is no affair of ours, you know. Poor uncle Crisp, it appears, approved of this Harry Jobson."

" Well, Robert, I suppose I must tell thy father sooner or later."

" And the sooner the better."

" No doubt," continued Mrs. Fisher, with a sigh. " I should never have thought, though, that Sarah would own a sweetheart that was shut up in jail."

" I should have despised her if it had been otherwise, mother," replied Robert, emphatically. "None of us can be secure from adversity, you know."

Mrs. Fisher told her husband all about the affair that night, and, as Robert had predicted, he made but few remarks. All he said was to warn his son not to drive the pony too hard, and look carefully at the harness, and to see that the ostler gave it a good bait of corn when they got to Bradford, which Robert promised him faithfully to see done.

Mrs. Fisher, on her part, contributed a large basket of sandwiches, bread and cheese, and a couple of bottles of her elder wine for Sarah's refection on the road, together with a smaller one for her son, in case he should be hungry on the road, either on going or returning, and Sarah being furnished with the address of the widow who lived in York, the two set out on their journey, Mrs. Fisher shouting out all kinds of warning after them until they were out of hearing.

It was noon when they approached Braidsworth, which looked very dull and deserted to

Sarah's eyes, as they drove up the straggling street of the village.

The house the Crisps had lived in was already inhabited, for there were six or eight dirty-looking children playing about the doorway, screaming and fighting, as ill-taught children always do. Sarah thought of poor little Jessie, sitting on a small stool on that door-step, as she had done the last time the child was well enough to go out, and the sight of these quarrelsome children, with torn garments and dirty flesh, brought the tears into her eyes in a moment.

"If you'll drive up to the Rectory gate, cousin, I'll get down and go up to the house by myself, "she said, trying to speak calmly. "I do so hope Dr. Vinen will be at home, then I shall have no trouble."

"It's too soon to bait the pony yet," thought Robert, "and so it's no use taking him out. You won't be long, Sarah," he said, aloud.

"Not more than five or ten minutes. You might drive slowly to the top of the village and then we can call and see if Mrs. Jobson is at home; she may want to send something to her son, you know."

"Well thought of, Sarah." Robert gave the pony a slight touch with the whip as his cousin turned up the neat gravel walk. "I shall expect you in ten minutes, mind."

And he was soon out of sight.

"Dr. Vinen is not at home," said the footman, in answer to poor Sarah's enquiry; "the family all left the Rectory for the south only yesterday, and will not be back for a week."

"Do you know if Squire Pearson is at home?" she ventured to ask before she turned away.

"Can't say at all, my good girl. Stay, I'll ask Mrs. Blewitt," he kindly added, on noticing the disappointment her pale face exhibited. "Come in and sit down till I come back."

Sarah sat in one of the hall chairs.

Mrs. Blewitt, the housekeeper, came to see who it was enquiring for her master. She was a kind-hearted creature, and suspected it must be some one in distress of one sort or another. As soon as she saw Sarah's pale thin face and slim figure, she came running along the passage, exclaiming—

"Why, Sarah, dear, what in the name of fortune brings you to Braidsworth this morning? Heart alive! but I am truly sorry the Rector is not at home. Is there anything I can do for you, my dear child?"

"Not much, I am afraid, Mrs. Blewitt. I wanted to see the Rector, but the man-servant told me he went from home yesterday for a week."

"He did, my lass. Come into my room and have a cup of tea or a glass of wine," said the kind-hearted housekeeper, with a tone of commiseration. "Dear! dear! how very thin you are grown."

Sarah's sad smile did not deny the charge, but recollecting that her cousin Robert would be getting fidgetty, she drew her shawl about her and rose to go.

" I am very sorry, Mrs. Blewitt, I cannot stop, as I have someone waiting for me," Sarah said. " Perhaps you can tell me if Squire Pearson is at home."

" Yes, for certain he is, for I saw him ride up the village not much more than five minutes ago," answered Mrs. Blewitt, at once divining the cause of Sarah's call. If it's any justice business you will find him in now. " Oh ! my dear child, how sorry I am for you that Dr. Vinen is not at home. Squire Pearson is terribly harsh with poor people."

" Terrible as he may be," said Sarah, sadly, " I must face him. I want to get a justice's order to see a friend of mine in York Castle, and I must have it."

" If it's Harry Jobson, my lass, you are going to see, give my love to him, and tell him that in spite of judge and jury, nobody in Braidsworth will believe that he had anything to do with the burning of Mr. Gladstone's foundry. Stay, you shall take him something from me," and the kind-hearted creature ran off much more quickly than her size would have seemed to permit.

She came back the next minute with a large spice loaf and a cream cheese, for the manufacture of which she was very celebrated. These she thrust into Sarah's hand, and giving her a hearty kiss, suffered her to depart at once.

Robert was as impatient and fretful as any embryo artist or disappointed lover could be, but his cousin bore his complaints in silence until they arrived at Mrs. Jobson's cottage, which they found shut up and deserted.

" She's at York with Harry," cried Sarah eagerly. " Please, Robert, drive to Squire Pearson's house, and then we'll get out of Braidsworth as quickly as we can."

" I wish I was clear of this affair," thought Robert, out of temper; then, as he caught sight of poor Sarah's sorrowful face, his heart smote him for the selfish feeling, and he set himself the task of cheering his fellow traveller in the best way he was able.

Sarah jumped down at the lodge and asked if the Squire was at home. The lodge-keeper's wife, after a time, said he was, and not without a strange palpitation at the heart did the poor girl, for the first time, set foot within the precincts of the justice's grounds.

For the last eight years this gentleman had not prospered as his pride told him he ought to have done ; and being by nature of a very gloomy, tyrannical disposition, his own disappointments had soured his temper to such a degree that the poor people in the neighbourhood had began to dread the consequence of his interference with their concerns. He had always been rather harsh upon the bench, perhaps more so than he would have been had he not got it into his head that his brother-magistrate, Dr. Vinen, was culpably lenient, and thus the character he enjoyed in this respect may readily account for the great terror with which Sarah sought the approaching interview.

Sarah wondered, when she came in sight of

the house, how people could say that the
Squire was poor, with such a grand house,
that was more like some fine picture, standing in its beautiful gardens, backed by fine
old trees. She had never seen a gentleman's
residence before, for she had rarely been many
miles from Braidsworth, and Mr. Pearson
guarded his domains with so much jealous
care that few but the gentry ever penetrated
so far into his grounds as to be able to catch
a glimpse of the mansion itself.

Whilst she was viewing its beauties and
wishing that it did not look quite so proud
and imposing, for then she thought she should
not feel so much afraid, she heard some one
behind her, and looking round perceived a
sour looking, dark man with two or three
dogs at his heels, and a gun over his shoulder,
coming towards her.

At first she thought him to be the game-
keeper, but on looking again she recognised
the Squire himself. He was not above the

middle height, but was stout built, and looked as if he could stand a vast amount of fatigue, if feeling it were necessary.

" Well, my girl, what has brought you here ?" he asked, in no pleasant tone, kicking one of the dogs out of his way, as he came near Sarah. "I know your face I think. What is your name ?"

" Crisp, sir," answered Sarah, dropping a timid curtsey.

" Crisp, eh ? Well, Miss Crisp, and what do you want ?" accompanying the question with the same haughty look.

" I came, sir, to ask the favour of your granting me a visiting order," said the timid girl, somewhat regaining her composure.

" For what purpose, may I ask ?" said her interrogator, leaning on his gun, and scanning her care-worn face with the air of a connoisseur of female beauty. " It is past justice hours, as, no doubt, you are aware."

" I should not have troubled you, sir, had

Dr. Vinen been at the Rectory," said Sarah firmly, " but as he has left home for a week I had no alternative."

" Oh ! you went to Dr. Vinen, did you ?" said he almost savagely, for there was an old grudge against Dr. Vinen rankling in his mind.

" I am very well known to Dr. Vinen, sir."

" Upon my word, Dr. Vinen ought to be very proud of the acquaintance," continued the magistrate. " Well, and for what do you want the order ?"

" To see some one who is confined in York Castle, sir," said Sarah.

" What is the person's name, Miss Crisp ?" he asked.

" Harry Jobson, sir."

" The young fellow charged with setting fire to Mr. Gladstone's foundry. Is he a relative of yours, pray ?"

" He is not, sir," said Sarah, whose temper, gentle, as it usually was, was beginning to give way under such petty annoyances. "I hope, sir, you will not detain me longer, as time is of great consequence to me."

"Don't be in such a hurry, my good girl. I wish to know, if Jobson is not a relative, what connection there is between you and him."

"I cannot explain it to you, sir," and Sarah blushed scarlet.

"Ah! I see! The old tale over again," said the magistrate, shouldering his gun and resuming his walk towards the house. "You can follow me," he added, looking over his shoulder at Sarah, who seemed scarcely to know whether to advance or retreat.

The poor girl thought it would be the best thing she could do to follow him as he desired, and did so at a respectful distance.

"Sit down here for a few minutes," he said, in his cold, haughty manner, on entering the hall. "Turn those dogs out, if you please, and shut the door on them."

He spoke as if he expected to be obeyed.

Sarah drove the dogs out, and shut the door on them as she had been desired. The Squire then strode across the hall, and opened another door, which, apparently, belonged to his library, judging from the numerous bookshelves she caught a transient glimpse of. In less than five minutes he came out again with a paper in his hand, which he thrust unceremoniously into her hand.

" There, Sarah Crisp—that, I think, you told me was your name—take that to the Castle, and they will admit you at once. Mind the dogs don't bite you as you go out; they don't like strangers," and with this encouraging caution he returned to the library again, and slammed the door behind him.

The three large rough dogs had all this time been leaping and barking outside. Sarah had never been afraid of dogs, and she did not hesitate for a moment to unbolt the door, although she fully anticipated a little rough usage from them.

"Down, Threadneedle! Down, Nelson!"

cried the magistrate's deep voice, as he came from the library. " Let them come in if they wish it," and Sarah admitted the dogs and liberated herself at the same time.

" Well, Sarah, you haven't hurried yourself," said her cousin, as she came up to the gate again. " I began to think of having a dig into the meat pasty mother put into the basket, I felt the time hanging so very heavy on my hands."

" I've got the order to admit me to the gaol, cousin, and that will account for the long time you've been kept," cried Sarah, as she clambered into the cart again.

" That's all right," said Robert, a little appeased.

" Yes, Robert, as you say—that's all right; but I really believe that if I had all the annoyance and indignities to meet over again, I'd rather walk bare foot to York than face that grim, haughty Squire again."

" Is he such a brute as all that, Sarah?" asked her cousin.

"He's worse, Robert. He taunts you with your misfortunes in a way that almost drives you mad?" cried Sarah, with a quivering lip. "Oh! it's much too bad, isn't it, cousin?"

"Yes; but it's no uncommon thing with grand people to conduct themselves in that way to their inferiors, Sarah," said Robert, philosophically.

"Then they ought to know better," returned Sarah, sadly.

"They'll be taught that," continued Robert, "if they don't take steps to put down the Unionists. These strikes will ruin the masters, impoverish the honest, hard working man, and what's worse, they'll send the work out of the country."

"Yes," returned Sarah, "that was my poor father's opinion. He often told Harry, he and the rest of the Unionists, if they were not put down by the strong arm of the law, would bring ruin upon themselves, upset the House of Lords, destroy the Church, and end in Republicanism."

" Ah ! it was a sad day for Jobson when he joined the Union."

" It has, indeed, proved so," said Sarah, sadly.

" Now, Sarah, suppose we put the pony into a trot, or we shall not catch the coach."

" I used to think it a very pleasant walk into Bradford when poor father was alive," said his companion, when they were fairly on the high road, " but trouble somehow prevents one enjoying pleasures."

" The feeling will come back, Sarah," said Robert. " Don't you think that tree and the gable end of that house would make a very pretty picture ?"

" You will be a great artist some of these days, cousin," said Sarah.

Robert heaved a deep sigh, as he said, sadly—

" I fear not, Sarah ; it is so very difficult now-a-days to excel in any profession."

" Why ?"

" Because there are so many first-rate artists to contend against."

"I'm sure you'll never be a second-rate one, Robert."

"I would cut my hand off first, my lass. If I found I could not attain the position I aim at as an artist, I'd plough and sow and reap as my father did before me."

"A very pleasant fate, too, cousin; far pleasanter than mine, for instance, will ever be."

"I suppose, Sarah, you love Harry Jobson very much," said Robert, after a pause, during which Sarah had been trying hard to prevent her tears being observed by her cousin.

"Yes, Robert," said she, blushing.

"Through evil report and good report."

"I do, and I shall always love him, cousin. How happy we should be with such a home as yours."

Robert sighed again to himself, and wished they were at Bradford; the journey had never seemed so long before.

Long or short, they got there at last, and then the noise and uproar of the streets prevented any further conversation. Sarah was thankful for this, as such colloquies as they had just had always pained her ; and she was not sorry either to find, on reaching the inn the coach started from, that it was on the point of leaving. She had, in fact, scarcely time to pay her fare and drink a little brandy and water with her cousin before the coachman came and told her to take her seat at once.

It was late in the afternoon when the coach arrived at the fine old city of York, the stately Minster of which had been visible for several miles before they drove through its quiet streets and reached the Market Place, where the coach drew up.

" Come my lass, don't stand there as if thou wast lost," said the guard kindly, as Sarah remained on the pavement, at a loss to decide which way to turn. " If thou hast friends in York thou expects to meet thee, go into the tavern and stay a bit till they come. Mrs. Johnson, there, will give you a cup of hot tea, I'll be bound."

" That I will, and welcome," said the

comely landlady, who had just come to the door. " Walk in, my dear, and wait till your friends come for you."

" If you could direct me to —— Gate, ma'am, I should feel very much obliged to you," said Sarah.

" Our Boots shall go with you as soon as ever he is at liberty, my dear," said the hostess, turning into the house. " We are just going to take our tea in the bar, so just step in."

The bar was certainly a very snug little place; so small that when eight or ten people took their seats, it looked quite crowded. The landlord sat near the fire-place; he was short and stout, and what is generally called " comfortable looking;" he was listening, or affected to be listening, to the grumblings of a very old woman, evidently—from the likeness between them—his mother; two or three boys and girls, who stared rudely at Sarah, and as many children under the charge of a domineering nurse of middle-age, whom they called Jemima, filled up the group.

"Take off your things, my dear, and draw up to the fire," said the landlady, kindly, "you've come a long way to-day, I should say?"

"From Chilworth, ma'am," was Sarah's quiet rejoinder.

"Then I'm sure you will stand in need of a good cup of tea before you set off to walk to —— Gate. I suppose you intend remaining in York some time?"

"I really do not know," said Sarah, "a week perhaps, at the farthest."

"You must contrive, somehow or other, to stay over Sunday, and attend the service at the Minster. I'm quite sure the singing would be a great treat to you."

"I certainly shall stay over Sunday, if I can. Do you know, ma'am, if anyone has come for me?"

"No."

"Then, perhaps, you will kindly allow some-one to go with me to show me the way.

"Poor lass, let Boots go with her," whispered one of the girls, on whom Sarah's pale, anxious face had made a favourable impression. " I am sure she wishes to be gone."

The landlady was of the same opinion, and so Boots was despatched with her to —— Gate, to seek out the widow, Mrs. Maxwell, whom Mrs. Fisher had mentioned to Sarah as the best person to take up her abode with whilst she remained in York.

Had Sarah's mind not been oppressed by the painfulness of her situation, she might have admired the gaunt, old-fashioned buildings, that presented themselves to her notice at every turn in the narrow streets she traversed, for no town in the kingdom, with the exception, perhaps, of Chester, excels York in the variety of its street architecture; but now it was her greatest anxiety to get to her resting-place, and be quiet for a short time. She knew that she would not be admitted to see Harry until the morning.

CHAPTER IX.

"I should think, miss, this would be the place you want to be at," said Boots, after they had crossed the Ouse-bridge. "If it's Mrs. Maxwell you want, she lives here, so good-night."

Sarah knew well enough Boots expected something for his trouble, so taking from her scanty store a sixpence, she gave it him, and turned to examine the outside of her new friend's house.

Her survey was sufficiently assuring. It was a small house, with a door painted green, and adorned with a brass knocker; and the room on the ground floor was evidently a sitting-room, for there were muslin curtains visible behind the blind, and a few plants in pots, which made it look summer-like to Sarah's country notions. There were two small windows above, partly let into the roof, with blinds as white as snow; and the whole aspect of the place was so encouraging that Sarah knocked at once.

A very tall, gaunt, scraggy woman answered the summons.

"Who do you want?" she asked, looking hard at Sarah.

"Mrs. Maxwell, ma'am," said Sarah, imagining her to be the servant, although she had not expected to find that Mrs. Maxwell kept a servant. "I have a message to give her from Mrs. Fisher, of Chilworth."

"Step in, if you please," said Mrs. Maxwell, with the same grave austerity; and she led the way up to the parlour, which felt exceedingly cold and chill, even on that warm autumn night.

Sarah's eye took in at a glance the stiff,

straight-backed chairs, with black horse-hair seating, placed against the walls—the meagre-looking table, in the middle of the room, that looked as if it never groaned beneath the weight of a good dinner—the scanty threadbare carpet, placed in the centre of the room, leaving the well-polished boards visible at the sides—and the curiously carved walnut-tree press that stood opposite the fire-place—all of which spoke of great thrift and careful husbanding of means, that were probably of the scantiest, even when made the most of; and then she wondered how she could have been deceived into expecting to find Mrs. Maxwell hearty and pleasant tempered like her aunt Fisher. She knew in a moment that the gaunt, hard-featured woman standing over her was the mistress of the house.

" I believe you know Mrs. Fisher very well, ma'am," said Sarah, looking steadily into that wrinkled face, " my aunt told me you were girls together."

" You are Helen Fisher's niece, then, are

you ?" she enquired, in her harsh, deliberate tones.

" I am, ma'am."

" Well; and pray what has brought you to York ?" she demanded.

" I have business here which may detain me three or four days, and as neither my uncle nor his son, my cousin Robert, could accompany me, Mrs. Fisher ventured to name you to me as a likely person to afford me shelter as long as I am detained."

" I suppose your aunt was anxious that you should be placed under the care of some respectable housekeeper."

" She was, ma'am," replied Sarah, " and as you were the only friend she had here, she made bold to hope you would do me that kindness."

" Is that all the luggage you have brought?" asked Mrs. Maxwell, glancing, as she spoke, to the small carpet bag Boots had carried under his arm.

" I only intend staying a very short time,

as I told you, ma'am," said Sarah, " and that will be quite enough to supply my simple wants."

Even Mrs. Maxwell's cold heart could not withstand Sarah's pleading looks. Almost insensibly her manner began to warm towards her, although she still retained a great portion of the blunt, cold manner she had of acting and speaking.

"I am afraid you find this room chilly," she said, on noticing how pale Sarah looked ; " my kitchen will be much more comfortable."

" I should be very glad to get near a fire to warm myself," said Sarah, shivering in spite of herself ; " the nights are getting very chilly now."

" Come along with me, then," said Mrs. Maxwell, " I rarely light a fire in this room, it smokes so; but my kitchen is really very comfortable."

It was nothing to compare with the Chilworth kitchen, for it was deficient in all the warmth and brightness of the latter. It was, however, scrupulously clean and neat—that cold kind of neatness which somehow annoys one more than all the dirt and slatternliness in the world can do.

A mere handful of fire lay smouldering in the grate. This Mrs. Maxwell, by some extraordinary process, stirred into a flickering blaze, that threatened every moment to expire, and then seating herself bolt upright in her arm-chair, she proceeded to examine Sarah as to the worldly position of her old friend Mrs. Fisher; what sort of character her husband was, and the number of their children. On the last point alone could Sarah enlighten her to her satisfaction, for she knew little of her uncle's means, and was not skilful enough to sketch his character, even had he possessed one, which we do not think was the case.

At nine o'clock she brought out a ponderous Bible, which she placed reverently on the table, directing at the same time an enquiring glance at her guest.

" I have always been accustomed to hear the Bible read at home," said Sarah with a faltering voice.

" It is almost the only solace I have left, my dear," said Mrs. Maxwell, as a tear trembled in her eyes, and she began to read from the Prophecies of Jeremiah with much better taste than her companion could possibly have expected. After she had read three chapters she closed the book, and wound up the evening's devotion with a somewhat long prayer.

By this time poor Sarah felt very sleepy and tired, and was not sorry when her hostess asked if she would like to go to bed.

" It is only a very humble place I can offer you, but, at any rate, the bed is clean, and the sheets as white as new fallen snow, and as sweet as soap and water could make them," she said with unwonted kindness, as she preceded Sarah into a place not much bigger than a tolerable sized closet, containing a bed and a single chair.

Sarah was thankful even for that, and as Mrs. Maxwell withdrew she flung herself on her knees, and notwithstanding the long prayer she had just listened to, poured out her soul in thankfulness to God. Then she arose, and undressing herself slipped into bed, and ere many minutes was in a sound sleep.

All through that unhappy night, Harry Jobson's image was present to her, and Harry's voice, mingling with that of Mrs. Maxwell, rang perpetually in her ears, when completely worn out, she sunk into an uneasy slumber, from which she did not awake until it was daylight.

Sarah got out of bed and dressed herself as quickly as possible, and went down stairs, fearing her hostess would be angry with her for being so late. She met Mrs. Maxwell at the bottom of the stairs, who, after bidding her good morning, said—

" I hope you have had a good night's rest. I did not call you when I got up, as I thought, after your journey yesterday, you would be quite tired out."

" I hope I have not kept you waiting break-fast for me, ma'am," said Sarah, stealing a stealthy look at the breakfast table.

" No, not at all. Shall we ask a blessing before we begin ?"

The blessing was invoked, and they sat down in silence to their meal. Poor Sarah could with difficulty swallow a single cup of tea, and she had scarcely any appetite, whilst her companion distressed her by frequent apologies for the poor fare she was enabled to offer, which unquestionably was scanty enough.

Sarah felt very uneasy, lest Mrs. Maxwell should propose accompanying her about the city, so she took the earliest opportunity of saying—

"I have an appointment this morning to meet a friend, which I very much fear will prevent my returning in time for your dinner, ma'am; so I hope you will have the goodness not to wait a minute for me."

Mrs. Maxwell's face changed in a moment to a frown, and she looked suspicious; but whatever she thought she made no remark.

The minute breakfast was over, Sarah arose and went up-stairs to put on her walking-dress.

" How very sad and pale she looks," was the widow's thought, as she heard Sarah's light foot upon the stairs. " Oh! my good and merciful God! I hope this young girl is not on the high road to her everlasting ruin! Why should such a sweet face be clouded over with trouble, if the undertaking she is engaged in is not wrong in the sight both of God and man?"

So troubled was she with these sad reflec-tions, that when Sarah came down again, equipped for her walk, she placed her hand on the girl's arm, and said, in an anxious tone—

"My dear child, I sincerely trust you have the approval of your own conscience in the matter that brought you to this place."

" I have, ma'am," Sarah replied, somewhat startled at her earnest manner, and suspecting that by some means or other she had learned what the object in her coming to York really was. "I am going to meet a friend who is in grievous trouble."

" Then may the blessing of God rest upon you!" said Mrs. Maxwell, with great earnestness, and, kissing Sarah, she permitted her to depart on her way without another word.

During the long walk to the Castle, Sarah had time enough to bring her rebellious thoughts into something like subjection. She went up to the gloomy-looking entrance, and knocked tremulously at the wicket. The gate-keeper asked her business.

" I want to see Harry Jobson, who is a prisoner here."

" Have you got a magistrate's order for admission?" asked the man.

"Yes," and Sarah displayed her order with greater confidence than she anticipated being able to do.

The gate-keeper opened a small door, and bade her enter.

"Sit down, my girl," he said, kindly, "and wait till there is a turnkey at liberty."

Sarah sat down to wait as patiently as she could, although now that she was so near the object of her devoted love, it seemed very cruel to keep her in suspense a moment longer than it was absolutely requisite.

Whilst she was waiting, an old woman, dressed in faded weeds, came in, with that air of hopeless grief upon her countenance that fills one with sorrow to witness.

"Always too soon, Mrs. Jobson," said the gate-keeper, smiling. "You were a quarter too early yesterday morning."

"I want to be with my boy," said the poor woman, with a faint blush, "and the clock always deceives me."

It was so dark a place, even at noon-day,

that Mrs. Jobson could not clearly distinguish Sarah's features, as she stepped forward into the middle of the room, and took her hand.

"I have come to see Harry, mother," said she, using the old familiar term of endearment, and immediately they were in each other's arms, shedding bitter tears.

"It's always the way with you women folk," said the man, in a somewhat contemptuous tone; "two of you cannot meet or part without so much hugging and blubbering, that it's quite ridiculous. I'd never marry if only just for that."

"You must bear with us, nevertheless," said Mrs. Jobson, drying her tears, and speaking more cheerfully, for the sight of Sarah Crisp had made her hopeful. "If you were in trouble like me or this dear girl, you would shed tears occasionally yourself."

"Maybe I might, mother," said he, more kindly. "However, you may go in now, I dare say."

"I have gone often enough to find the way

without the turnkey, Sarah," said Mrs. Jobson, taking her hand.

"I hope we haven't far to go," said Sarah, nervously, as a gang of prisoners came into the yard they were traversing, with mops and pails to cleanse it. "Some of these men look very terrible."

"They won't do us any harm, my love. Poor Harry scarcely ever leaves his cell; he feels the disgrace of being seen in company with such a disreputable set of wretched creatures, sorely. I'm afraid, my child, you'll find him sadly altered."

"He will think the same of me, mother, for I feel that I am very much changed since he left us."

"Young folks don't take trouble as they ought," said Mrs. Jobson. "Now, my love, take hold of my dress, so that I may have my arm free to climb the stairs," and she began to ascend in total darkness a very steep stone staircase, which led to her son's cell.

"Stop just for a minute," whispered her

companion, as they reached a gallery which was partly lighted by narrow loopholes in the wall, and which had many iron-sheathed doors opening into it, "my mind is in such a perfect whirl that I should only frighten Harry, going into his cell in this condition. Now," after a short pause, "I am ready," and Mrs. Jobson, walking first, ushered her into the cell, with the words—

"Harry, my dear, good lad, here is Sarah Crisp."

"I thought, Sarah, dear, you had forgotten me," were the first words he uttered, as Sarah sunk into his arms. "Many and many a weary hour have I sat on my bed here, listening to every footfall that sounded on the stairs."

"Expecting it was mine, Harry?" said Sarah, the tears falling down her cheeks.

"Yes, my dear lass. I did not know how severely you had been tried yourself, or I would not have watched and waited as I did."

" Dear Harry—"

" Mother," said her son, interrupting Sarah. " you must leave us for a few minutes to ourselves," and as Mrs. Jobson went out, without a murmur, Harry placed Sarah on the only chair the cell could boast, and seating himself on the iron stock of his bed, with both her hands clasped in his, required her first to tell him all that had happened to herself since they parted.

Whenever she began to cry he put his arm round her neck and begged her to take courage again, and so, after many interruptions, Sarah got to the end of her sad tale, with her description of the journey from Chilworth, and her taking up her abode with the widow Maxwell. Then Harry described his own prison life, which was sad and mournful, and uneventful enough, even had not his trial loomed grim and black in the distance.

After this the lovers fell into less painful discourse, which must have been more interesting, for they quite forgot the poor mother pacing backwards and forwards in the gallery all this time, till at last Sarah's heart smote her with the recollection of Mrs. Jobson's pale sad face.

"It was very wicked of us to forget you, dear mother," she said, with the happy smile that made her pale face look almost beautiful, as she ran out and brought the poor old woman into the cell again. "Sit down between Harry and me, and let us talk over the future a bit."

"Ah! Sarah," said her lover, gloomily, "you forget that I am not free yet."

"No, Harry, I do not," Sarah rejoined, "but, please God, your innocence will be fully proved before long, and then we shall go back to dear Braidsworth again."

"I will never go back there again," said Harry, sternly.

"Then I will go wherever you and mother go," Sarah said, with much firmness; "death only shall part us."

"Bairns! bairns! it frets me to hear you

talk in that way," cried Mrs. Jobson, mournfully. " Your father and I, Harry, used to talk in that self same manner, like two silly, inexperienced things as we were, and within a year of our marrying he was laid in his last earthly home. He never lived to see his boy."

" You must not scold us," said Sarah, clinging to her and kissing the pale, wrinkled face, that told of years of grief and sorrow; " it is all we have to hope for at present."

" Don't you often recall those protestations my father made to you, mother, when he was a young man ?" asked her son, with simple earnestness, as he took his mother's hand. " In the still noon-day, when faint, worn with toil, you sit down for a few minutes to rest, does the old familiar voice never repeat those speeches in your ear ?"

" Sometimes, Harry; you know, I often hear him talking to me when I'm in bed," said the widow, very solemnly.

Harry did not smile at this proof of his mother's credulity, but contented himself with entreating that she would permit Sarah and himself to indulge in their reflections, and in their anticipations of the future, modest and humble as they were.

" I wish," said Sarah, looking round the bare and ugly walls with a cheerful smile, " I had brought the pastry and the elderberry wine aunt Fisher gave me when I left Chilworth. However, I can bring them to-morrow."

" What have you for dinner, mother?" asked Harry, abruptly. " You must both be hungry after your long walk."

" I wish, my lad, that you could take such a one; thou'rt getting as white as a sheet with being mewed up here."

" It will soon be over, mother."

"I hope so, my dear lad. Sarah, just stoop down and get that bit of cold meat from the bottom shelf. You see there's not much room here for a pantry, and we have just to manage these matters in the best way we can."

" Oh! it will do famously," said Harry,

trying to brave it out; "there's always been room as yet, except last Sunday, when you would bring such a quantity of bread and meat and potatoes that we had to stow half of them away under the bed. I'm afraid, Sarah, dear, we shall want that chair for a table on the present occasion. I can only repeat my mother's regret at the scantiness of my accommodation."

"We shall manage capitally," said Sarah, who was beginning to feel more and more at home every minute. "How many plates have you?"

"Only two; but that difficulty can soon be got over. You and I can eat off the same with a great deal of ease. Mother, will you ask God's blessing?"

Harry's face looked calmly solemn as the widow's feeble voice was heard imploring a benediction on what they were going to eat.

"Will you come and see me to-morrow, Sarah?" asked Harry, a couple of hours after they had finished their frugal repast, and as his mother and Sarah were going away. "I rarely ever open my lips to a human being but to the old woman there, so you may be sure my time hangs heavily enough on my hands."

"At eleven, Harry," said Sarah, struggling to disengage herself from him. "Now you must positively let me go."

"One moment more, my love," said Harry, still holding her. "I suppose you will write home to-night?"

"I promised I would."

"Who shall you write to?"

"Who should I write to, you silly fellow? Shall I write to Robert?"

"No, Sarah, don't."

She kissed him tenderly, although his mother was standing close by them, and without blushing, too, as if she felt there was no shame in the act.

"May I write to Robert, Henry?"

"If you wish it."

"But I don't wish it, and I won't write to

him. I love you far more dearly than fifty Roberts, and I won't write to him if it would pain you in the slightest degree in the world. I will write to aunt Fisher."

"That's a dear girl."

"And I will tell her she must not expect me back at Chilworth this week, at any rate," said Sarah, still holding his hand. "Mrs. Maxwell, I am sure, will give me house-room for that time or longer if requisite, and I will come every morning with your mother to see you. Now, good-bye, Harry."

The poor girl did go at last.

Every morning, true to her promise, she presented herself at the wicket along with Mrs. Jobson, and late in the afternoon they might be seen coming away again in company. The cynical gate-keeper soon discovered that on these occasions the widow could scarcely restrain her tears, whilst Sarah's face was once more becoming rosy and smiling.

"What extraordinary creatures these women are," he would say, scornfully, as he let them out. " The old woman is sorrowful enough, but the young lass laughs and giggles as if her sweetheart didn't stand as fair a chance as any man could do of going to the hulks."

He did not understand the cause of Sarah's happiness.

On the Saturday morning, however, when they came together as was their wont, Sarah looked as sorrowful as any human being could desire, so the man said—

" What's the matter now, my lassie ? I would rather see the pleasant looking smile you brought yesterday than that downcast look."

" She is going home again to-day," said Mrs. Jobson, answering for her; " there was a letter this morning."

" And bad news in it, I suppose," he said, bluntly.

" Not exactly that, though there was nothing good either. Can you not give her a chair till the clock strikes ?"

He pulled a form towards them, and said,

in his surly way, that they might sit down on that.

" The Assizes are drawing on fast now," he said, a moment after.

" I am glad to hear it," said Mrs. Jobson; " it is terrible for the poor lad to remain in prison."

" But worse slaving at the hulks," he added, nodding his head significantly, as if he thought Harry Jobson stood a very good chance of the latter fate. " They keep a tight look out there now."

The two poor helpless women longed heartily for the clock to strike, but the more they desired it the further distant it seemed, the hands moved so slowly.

" Will she be a witness?" he asked, jerking his finger in the direction of Sarah, who was sitting with her head buried in her hands, trying to nerve herself to bear the parting with Harry calmly, for his sake.

" I cannot tell."

" Can't you?"

" No."

" Well, that's a pity."

" Why ?"

" Because she'd tell on the jury."

" Do you think so ?"

" I'm sure so, if she could be brought in as a witness in any way," he said, with professional significance. " She has such a winning kind of way with her that would be almost sure to get over most folk, and juries are generally very tender-hearted. I shouldn't be in the least afraid to take my chance if I could have her for a witness on my side."

" You think so," said Mrs. Jobson, repeating the words.

" I don't think about the matter. I am certain sure, ma'am, she'd tell wonderful on the jury !"

" I should be sorry to bring her before such a rabble," said the widow, tossing her head proudly.

" That's all very well ; but take my word, you'd find it worth your while to put her in the witness-box, ma'am," said the man, eagerly, without noticing the toss of the head. "Your son's case, I should say, is not over strong."

"My son will have no difficulty in proving his innocence," cried the widow, proudly; "and if he could not, I would not suffer that dear innocent child to go through such an ordeal. Come, lass," she said, addressing Sarah, "the clock has struck eleven," and she went forward, followed by Sarah.

"Well, well," soliloquised the gate-keeper, looking after them. "The pride of that old woman is wonderful, but she'd better have put it in her pocket on this occasion. The poor young thing! She would tell upon any jury."

"This will be our last meeting, Harry," Sarah said, as soon as they entered his cell. "I am obliged to go home to-day."

"What is the matter, Sarah?" asked Harry, anxiously, and with a very woe-begone countenance. "I thought you intended stopping here another week, at the least."

"My cousin Robert is ill," she said, trying to speak cheerfully, although the effort was exceedingly painful to her. "He is very bad, I fear, from what aunt Fisher says."

"You must go, I suppose?" added Harry, in a desponding tone. "Nobody but you, Sarah, can nurse him."

"That is not kind, Harry; I have already told you I do not feel for Robert as—as you know who, Harry."

"Don't try her too far, Harry," said Mrs. Jobson. "You know she's far from strong, and those kind of suspicions are worse to bear than anything else. Sarah is, and will continue to be, true to you, whatever falls out."

"It's very hard to bear, this mewing a man up like a caged tiger in a caravan, Sarah," said her lover, bitterly; "if they keep me here a month longer, I shall go mad. Can you not stop over to-day, at any rate?"

"I wish I could, Harry, but I must not," said Sarah, sobbing; "uncle is to meet me at

Bradford to-night. I will come back again as soon as ever Robert is better."

Harry threw himself upon the bed, and buried his face in his hands.

"What can I say?" whispered the young girl to the old woman, as a smothered sob or two became audible in the dead silence that ensued. "Oh! mother, this is, indeed, very hard to bear!"

"Be patient, my love; he will come round presently," said Mrs. Jobson, in the same tone; "these kind of outbursts never last long with him."

They remained very quiet for nearly ten minutes, watching the motionless figure lying before them, neither venturing to speak, and both busy with the sad thoughts that were passing through their minds. At last Mrs. Jobson said, as she placed her hand gently, with a mother's fondness, on her son's curly head—

"Harry, lad, you must bid Sarah good-bye."

He was at her side in a moment, with the tears still wet upon his flushed cheeks, and brimming over in his eyes.

"God bless you, my poor little Sarah," he said, wildly, as he kissed her lips over and over again. "You must not think of me at Chilworth as you have seen me at parting. Don't think of my being in gaol at all, but think of me as I used to be, when we rambled in Braidsworth wood, long, long ago, Sarah, when we were both happy, loving children!"

"When you used to plait rush caps for me, Harry," said Sarah, smiling through her tears; "it was all sunshine then, I think, when we were children."

"It shall be all sunshine again, Sarah. I am strong and hopeful now," and he drew himself proudly up, as if the narrow place he stood in was the free wild forest with the heavens for its canopy. "I will not allow the future to darken my mind with its shadows; or if they come, dear love, I will invoke your image to chase them away. Again, God

Almighty bless you !" and with one more long embrace they parted.

The widow saw her to the coach. Sarah begged that she would tell Harry to write very often, for she had forgotten it at parting with him. Mrs. Jobson readily promised that she would do so, and Sarah watched her thin, wasted figure standing at the corner of Coney Street until the coach made a turn and hid her from view.

Sarah's thoughts were so engrossed during the whole journey that it was only when the coach arrived at Bradford she knew the journey was over by hearing the people about her say so, as the coach rattled over the stones of the town. Had they travelled all night Sarah would have been none the wiser, for a kind of stupor had taken possession of her mind, and she only felt what a relief it would be to lie down and die.

" Mind how you get down, Sarah," said a familiar voice, as on turning round to descend from the coach she felt herself hugged by a pair of strong arms, which soon placed her on the ground. "Like myself, I think thou'rt not much accustomed to riding outside coaches and such like machines."

"Oh! Uncle Fisher, is that you?" exclaimed Sarah, as she caught a glimpse of his ruddy looking face. "And how is Robert?"

"Very bad, lass."

"Oh! dear, how sorry I am to hear that," said the poor girl, sorrowfully. "I did hope that I should have left all my trouble behind me at York."

"There's more to come yet," said Mr. Fisher, doggedly; "but come, get up into the cart."

And he lifted his niece unceremoniously into that humble vehicle.

CHAPTER X.

By the middle of that week Mr. Gladstone and his sisters had become settled in their new abode at Bradford, and William had entered upon his employment. Kate, and Frances, and Hannah had managed everything so well that neither Sophia nor her brother felt the change from their old to their new residence so keenly as they would have done had there been that want of management and order which accompanies so many changes of residence.

It was certainly strange for the first few days that they could not see the Rectory and the garden when they came down to breakfast; but by degrees this wore off, and Sophia began to look for spots in the new landscape, that lay stretched out before her window, with the same interest that new objects always excite in us when those objects are neither painful nor obnoxious to our feelings.

In another week Frances' school was formally commenced by the arrival of five pupils, two of whom were brought by Mrs. Vinen, and the other three were strangers.

" You must have felt very strange, Frances," said her brother one night, when they were assembled in Sophia's room, which looked quite as bowery with exotics as ever her old one at " The Rookery " had done. " Very strange indeed you must have felt with those five gawky girls I caught a glimpse of, as I came home to-night."

" Not more so, William, than you did when first taking employment under Mr. Saunders," was Frances' quiet answer. " You must have felt the change far more keenly."

"I felt it keenly enough, certainly, Frances,"

said her brother; "but the feeling soon wore off. It was assuredly very trying when Mr. Macintosh—an old customer of mine, you remember—first came in to the office to order some bolts."

"What did you do, William?"

"Looked like a fool for a minute, and then felt like a man who had no cause for shame the next. Macintosh's hearty grasp of the hand drove such silly pride and false sentiment out of my head for ever."

"And you took his order?"

"To be sure I did, and have never had a recurrence of the foolish pride since. I hope, Frances, you got as quickly out of your dilemma?"

"Not quite; indeed, brother, it has scarcely gone yet, for a feeling of strangeness comes over me every now and then, when I hear Mary Templeton's singularly harsh voice blundering through her lesson in history in a way that would drive Hume mad, or have to look my disgust at the merciless manner in which poor Emily Simpkin massacres 'The Battle of Prague' on my piano."

"Simpkin stopped and shook hands with me to-day," said William. "I like his hearty, frank way very much. He said his wife and he would probably drop in to-night."

"And that is their knock," said Kate, jumping up. "They may as well come up here, Frances."

Hannah, apparently, was of the same opinion, for she ushered them up without the slightest ceremony, and they were in the room almost as soon as our little party knew they were in the house.

Mr. Simpkin came first, a bluff, stout, practical looking man, with plenty of character in his fresh, good-humoured looking face, and still more in his Yorkshire voice and dialect. He looked well, even beside Mr. Gladstone, although there was nothing of the gentleman in his appearance, and this struck them all at the same moment in the way he shook hands with each of them, and bade them welcome to Bradford. No one but a man who had been used to rough it in the world would have grasped the ladies' hands so tightly, nor would any gentleman have uttered the clumsy but unabashed speech he did when Frances handed him a chair.

Mrs. Simpkin did not please any of them half so much; she was commonplace both in figure and manner, without any of her husband's shrewd, keen sense to atone for these deficiencies. Very stout and very short she assuredly was, and perhaps good-natured as well, judging by her fair, fat face; but somehow all began to wonder, after the first five minutes, how the clever man of business could have linked his fate with a woman of such a negative sort of character as Mrs. Simpkin evidently possessed.

" You must find a great change, ladies," said Mr. Simpkin, after the ceremonies of intro-duction had been got through. " Bradford isn't like Braidsworth after all, is it ?"

" Not exactly, sir," Miss Gladstone replied.

" Just so ; there's more smoke, and dirt, and noise in Bradford. I told my mistress that, when we first came to settle down here ; but it was into a far worse place than this we had to put our heads, I promise you."

He said this with a kind of honest pride that became him well. Mr. Simpkin never forgot how he had worked his way up from a close, disagreeable back street, adjoining the principal iron works, to the pretty airy house in which he now resided; he liked rather to remind his wife of this fact, who sometimes stood in danger of forgetting it.

Mrs. Simpkin seemed annoyed.

" Folks with perhaps twenty-five or thirty shillings a week, Mr. Gladstone, can't pick and choose their houses like their betters,' said he, turning his square, broad-looking head round to where William sat. "I pay almost as much now for house-rent up here."

Mrs. Simpkin blushed, and looked vexed, but her blushes and vexed looks had no effect upon her husband; he had no patience with her silly, false pride, as he called it. He had received a good plain education, and that was all his father had ever given him; what he had earned he owed to the goodness of God and his own industry. They must have married very early, for Simpkin himself could not be more than thirty-five years of age, and their eldest daughter was a great girl of eleven or twelve at the least.

"How does our lass get on?" asked Mr. Simpkin, addressing Frances, who he knew was her preceptress. "Only slowly, I'm afraid; she doesn't want for brains neither, and in the main she's not a bad girl."

"I have no fault to find with her; she is very attentive," said Frances, who was beginning to be pleased with his blunt, straightforward way of talking and thinking. "Patience, you know, Mr. Simpkin, is an essential ingredient in a teacher."

"Very true. You are too young, miss, I should suppose, to be blessed with much of that," he said, thinking how pleasantly she spoke, and how unlike most of the school-mistresses she appeared ; and he continued "one must get a few ups and downs in the world, to learn that valuable gift, I take it."

"I hope you will teach Emily music and drawing, Miss Gladstone," interposed Mrs. Simpkin.

"I hope you'll do nothing of the kind, just at present, Miss Gladstone," said Simpkin, emphatically. "Let her be well grounded in grammar, in writing, and the use of figures, but, above all, get her well up in grammar, for without that, education is like building a house without a solid foundation, the superstruc-ture will soon tumble down. Yes, miss, ground the lass well in grammar, and after that we can talk of music and drawing, and such like acquirements such as my mistress wishes. It's all a mistake polishing up young folk before they've had the requisite foundation laid to enable them to make their way in the world."

"You are quite right, Mr. Simpkin," said Mr. Gladstone.

"I'm glad to hear you say so, Mr. Gladstone; you've been brought up in a good school. I can't bear the sham things at all, sir, as unnatural as wicked. Sailing under false colours, I say."

"All young ladies are taught music and drawing now, Mr. Simpkin," said his wife.

"Mine sha'n't at present," her husband said. "Teach them drawing, indeed! More need teach them how to make puddings and pies, or darn their father's and brother's stockings, my love. It makes me quite angry to think on't—but we didn't come here, Miss Gladstone, to talk about school; we came to be neighbourly, and to spend a pleasant hour or two, and I hope you'll come and see us in return, in a day or two, at furthest."

"Certainly, Mr. Simpkin," said Mr. Gladstone, "we wish to be neighbourly if we can."

"That's right, sir; you and I can talk

about the iron trade over our grog, whilst the ladies sew and talk scandal. You know I'm a founder myself, Mr. Gladstone."

Mr. Gladstone was quite aware of this, and he knew that Henry Simpkin's name stood high, both as a clever and honourable man of business, and who had worked his way up from a very humble station by hard work and thrift.

" That was a wonderfully fine situation of yours at Braidsworth, Mr. Gladstone," said Simpkin, who knew Braidsworth well, and had ofttimes envied William the possession of it. "Plenty of water-power there, sir; I suppose the ' run ' never gets dry, even in the hottest summer ?"

" Never."

" I'm very badly off that way," said Simpkin; "indeed, I've often wished I had those premises of yours."

" They were very convenient in many respects," said William.

" They made a very tidy bonfire at any

rate, Mr. Gladstone," said Simpkin, never for
a moment reflecting what amount of pain he
was inflicting upon his hearers. " Some day
we'll take a turn over and see the place. I
suppose you still hold the lease ?"

" Yes, I have half made up my mind to dispose of it, for a time," said Mr. Gladstone.

" Don't be in a hurry to do that, Mr.
Gladstone," said Simpkin, significantly.
" Wait a bit, you may make better terms
presently. It is such an out-and-out place
for water power, sir."

That same water power had haunted Simpkin's mind for a very long time. Often
when walking along the fields in a broiling
sun, in July or August, had he thrown himself down on his back, and pictured his own
foundry-yard transported to the side of one
of the clear trout streams that gleam in the
sunlight for many a mile round Braidsworth,
and many a sigh he suffered to escape him
when he thought of all this wealth of water
running to waste. It haunted him even when

sitting quietly in his counting-house, and his thoughts mingled with the clack of the foundry hammer. It came to him, too, in his night dreams, in the shape of a brawling, turbid stream, high up among the hills where he was born.

"On no account, Mr. Gladstone, dispose of the Braidsworth works in a hurry," repeated Simpkin, with great urgency. "When you do wish to get them off your hands come to me, and we'll see if we cannot strike some sort of a bargain. I'd give something handsome for the lease of that bit of land."

"But you have excellent premises of your own, Mr. Simpkin," said William, amused at his pertinacity.

"Well, Mr. Gladstone, I have, and I have not, as one may say. My foundry is handy enough for business, for it's in the middle of the town, but it's so confoundedly cramped for space. Why, you can hardly swing a cat in it, as the saying is, it's so very small."

He put forth his strong, vigorous arms, as

if he felt the confinement in a corporeal sense, and sighed, or rather groaned, after a fashion of his own, but though it was the groan of a prosperous man, it was a groan nevertheless.

"I will go over to see your works some day, if you will give me leave," said William.

"Do! I shall be right glad to see you, Mr. Gladstone. Come, wife, it's time we were on the move," and Mr. Simpkin arose and buttoned his coat.

"Mind what I say, Miss Gladstone," said he, turning to Frances, in his rough, determined tone, although the manner in which he held her hand was as kind as it was possible to be. "Don't teach my lass drawing, and you'll oblige me."

"I hope Mrs. Simpkin will call and talk the matter over with me," said Frances, escaping the snare he had laid for her. "I can, however, assure you, Mr. Simpkin, I am anxious to teach my pupils nothing but what will be advantageous to them."

"You are a sensible girl, my dear," he said

as he shook her hand. " Good night, ladies—
good night, miss !" and he backed out of the
room.

" What an extraordinary couple," exclaimed
Kate when they were gone. " Mr. Simpkin
with his 'just so,' and his loud voice and
vigorous way of thinking for himself, is
amusing."

" And you will like him after the first ten
minutes, Kate," said Frances, who had already
made up her mind to like him. " When the
first shock of having your hands almost
wrung off is over, and you can accustom
yourself to his originality, and his brusque-
ness, Mr. Simpkin's clear good sense and
kind nature come out wonderfully in comparison with the insipid mediocrity of his
vapid wife."

" Mrs. Simpkin is, I am afraid, insipid," said
Sophia, who had been engaged with her knitting all this time.

" I am sure she was disappointed when
she cast her eyes round the room," said Kate.

" I suppose she expected we could not afford good furniture now. How came a shrewd man of business to link himself to such a common-place creature ?"

" Love is blind, it is said, Kate," was Frances's quiet rejoinder.

" I have some faith in the proverb; but I don't think William would have thrown himself away in such a manner," said Kate.

" William has a refined taste, which Mr. Simpkin has not," said Frances, " a taste for the beautiful, an intellect that would prevent him from uniting himself with such a woman as Mrs. Simpkin.

" I suppose we shall have Mr. and Mrs. Jeremy next," said Kate, stealing a look at the clock. " Do you think, Frances," and she blushed, " that is William Wilding coming up the stairs with our brother ?"

" It is about his usual time," said her sister. " You must have a very keen sense of hearing though, Kate, to catch the sound, if there is one. I cannot hear anything."

Kate smiled and blushed again. She looked so happy, so confiding in her love for Wilding, that none of them could bear to cross her in the affection she could not help displaying, whenever his name was mentioned.

"I was sure I was right," she exclaimed, as the door opened and the truant Wilding entered. "Why were you so long in coming?" she cried, springing up like a startled fawn, wishing to fly to him, and yet kept back by the smile she saw on her brother's face.

"Why was I so long in coming, Kate?" echoed her lover, kissing her brow, and seating himself at her side, "because, simpleton, I am a man of business, and cannot call my time my own."

"A man of busines!" repeated Kate, who hated the term, "what can you be engaged with?"

"Brick and mortar, silly one; I am building," he replied.

"What are you building?"

" You must come and see for yourself, Kate, some day soon ; I can't tell you," answered Wilding gaily.

" I hope you are not pulling that beautiful old house down, at any rate," said Kate anxiously.

" Only a little bit. I am building a new dining room."

" Why so ; the old one was so snug and comfortable, a storm might be raging furiously outside and you would be none the wiser sitting there, half buried in those old-fashioned Turkey carpets of yours."

" One would really imagine, Kate, that you had a reversionary interest in Wilding's carpets," said her brother, sarcastically.

" So she has," said Kate's lover, turning his handsome face upon her. " If I thought my alterations would not give her pleasure I would kick every lubberly brick-layer and carpenter out of the place to-morrow."

" I am sure, William, I shall approve of

everything," said Kate gently. " We will drive over some early day to see your improvements."

" It must be some day, then, when I am in the way," said Wilding coaxing her to the piano. "Now let us try that duet over again."

" I believe we quarrelled over it the last time you tried it with me," said Kate, looking up into his face, as she ran her fingers over the keys. " I was very naughty then, dear William."

" Not naughty, love ; only self-willed ;" and their rich voices were heard blending in delicious harmony.

CHAPTER XI.

UNCLE FISHER was by no means a loquacious man, so Sarah did not wonder at his not speaking during their ride home. This knowledge of his character did not prevent her feeling uncomfortable in his company, for the most silent man in the world can find something to say when meeting, after an absence however short, any one he has been in the habit of associating with daily.

Sarah was anxious to hear about Robert ; she was perplexed at his sudden illness, and very uneasy about it as well, for she dreaded, without knowing why, that she was in some way the remote cause of his indisposition. A stone wall, however, could not be more impenetrable than was Mr. Fisher, when really and determinedly silent, as he evidently was on this occasion, so Sarah did not venture to ask him any questions about home, but sat unhappy and anxious, watching the road in front, and thinking it so long they never should get to their journey's end, their progress seemed so slow in comparison with the journey to Bradford a few days before.

At length it grew dark, and Sarah began to doze on her seat, for she was really weary with having travelled nearly the whole day. She did not think they were so near home when Mr. Fisher suddenly gave her a rough shake, and told her to open her eyes; a command she instantly obeyed.

There was Chilworth farmstead looming in front, whilst Bobby and Tommy stood out in the road as they had done the first night of their sister's arrival, holding up the stable lantern, which shed a long dull light along the road.

"Where is thy aunt, Bobby?" asked Mr. Fisher; opening his lips for the first time.

Bobby pointed up to his Cousin Robert's window, and ran up to the pony's head, whilst Mr. Fisher and Sarah got down as well as they could.

Mr. Fisher then ordered the two lads to come with him to the stable, and as the lantern, of course, went with them, Sarah was left in total darkness.

Stiff and weary, she was groping her way to the door, when a hand was so suddenly laid upon her dress, that she could scarcely help uttering a stifled scream.

"Pray don't play any tricks upon me," was her first exclamation, fancying it must be one of the village lads trying to frighten her; "if you do I shall call Mr. Fisher."

"Is that you, Sarah Crisp?" said some one in a voice so low that it was scarcely above a whisper, in answer to her trembling threat.

"It is, and pray who are you?"

"God knows I can scarcely tell you. I

must speak with you, however, Sarah Crisp, where no one can hear us. Do you not know me?" said the mournful voice.

"I think I do," said Sarah, trembling violently, for she had already recognised her half-sister's voice. "I thought, Fanny, you were dead."

"I wish the thought had been true, Sarah," said Fanny, with remarkable bitterness. "Did you wish me dead, Sarah?"

"I did not, Fanny. God forbid I should," was Sarah's truthful answer. "I have wept and prayed for you, sister, night and morning, for I thought the life you were leading must end sooner or later in misery to yourself; but I never laid such heavy guilt upon my soul as to wish you dead." Then, recollecting that Fanny must have come some distance, she said, "I dare not ask you into the house, Fanny, but if I can get you some meat—"

"I'm not hungry, Sarah," she interrupted; "it was neither for your meat nor your drink that I came here," said Fanny, clutching her arm. "Sarah Crisp, I must speak with you where there is no risk of anyone overhearing us."

Sarah thought of her own little room. It was next to the one occupied by Mr. and Mrs. Fisher, and the idea was at once rejected the instant it was formed. There was no other place about the house, and Mr. Fisher was in the habit of going round the stables and farm buildings at night whenever he heard the slightest noise. So she concluded it would be running too great a risk of detection to make an appointment for her to meet Fanny in any of the outbuildings.

"You used not to be a coward, Sarah," said Fanny, with something like contempt in the tone, misinterpreting her silence, "and surely you do not fear that I will do you any harm, bad as I am."

"I am not afraid, and I will meet you," said Sarah, promptly. "We must be quick, for I am afraid my uncle will find us here. Go up the lane till you come to a stile on your right hand. You will know it even in the dark, because uncle Fisher had it painted white for us to recognise easily in going backwards and forwards to the village of a dark night. Cross the stile and keep by the hedge side until you come to a barn, the door of which you will find open, for I was in it not more than a week ago."

" How long must I wait?"

" That is impossible for me to tell. Cousin Robert is very ill, and I probably may not be able to get away from him just at first, but I will come the first moment I can slip out of the room. Can I not bring you anything to eat?"

" I could not eat, lass, if you did," said Fanny, lifting herself up. " Hush! I hear some one coming."

" It must be uncle Fisher. For God's sake, Fanny, go away and remember my directions," whispered Sarah, in a tone of terror.

" I remember every word you have uttered, only be quick, for the night is very cold."

Fanny grasped Sarah's thin hand again and disappeared.

It was fortunately a false alarm as far as Mr. Fisher was concerned, and Sarah had time to steal into the kitchen without being heard, and change her dress before her uncle came in, accompanied by Bobby and Tommy.

" Things are not quite in the order they were when you left us, niece," said Mr. Fisher, glancing very despondingly round the kitchen, which was in a somewhat disorderly state, as he seated himself in his arm chair. " But thy aunt has been very much engaged of late, and has had but little time or opportunity of doing those kind of things. Go up, lass, and see Robert, though I've great doubts of your being able to do him any good."

The first glance at her cousin's pale, emaciated face, as he sat up in bed, propped up with pillows, was almost more than she could bear. Ill as Sarah had pictured him, in her own imagination, she had never dreamed that he could be so bad as he evidently was, and when the reality was forced upon her the poor girl could with difficulty restrain the sharp cry of pain that rose to her lips.

" Bring Sarah a chair, mother," said Robert, in his accustomed manner, although Sarah could, she fancied, hear a dash of sadness in the familiar tones that she had never noticed before. "Sit down beside me, cousin, and tell me everything."

" In the first place, Robert," said Sarah, as her gaze sunk beneath the power of his hollow, earnest eyes, " in one word, dear Robert, tell me what is the matter."

" I have been very ill, I suppose, my lass," was his calm reply; " very ill, by my mother's account."

" And the doctor's, Robert," said Mrs. Fisher, who was almost as much altered as her son, and looked years older even in that one short week. " Oh! you have been ill indeed, and—"

" Well, well, mother, let us forget that for

the present," said Robert, pettishly interrupting her. " Sarah, I think, will not be inclined to contradict what you assert, but for mercy's sake spare her listening to all the details."

" When was he taken ill ?" asked Sarah, in an undertone.

" The day after you left. I heard him pacing up and down his room nearly the whole of that night, Sarah, and when he came down to breakfast in the morning he looked badly indeed."

" All for want of my night's sleep, mother," said Robert, with an attempt at gaiety that made his ghastly look infinitely more striking.

" Oh! Robert, that is a tempting of Providence," exclaimed good Mrs. Fisher, in a tone of grief. " The illness was in your body all through that night, or you would have slept as well as you usually did."

" Well, well, mother, say no more about it. The doctor says I am quite out of danger, and as Sarah has come back you may breathe more freely again."

" I wish I could, Robert."

" Can you not persuade my cousin to sit down?" demanded her son; "the poor lass looks as if she'd drop."

" Thank you, cousin, I can find a seat my-self," said Sarah, without quitting her place by the bed. " I little thought when we parted the other day at Bradford that I should come back to find you in such a sad condition."

" It is God's will, my dear cousin. How did you leave Harry Jobson?" asked the poor invalid.

" Very unhappy, Robert. It's a dreadful misfortune to be shut up between stone walls, when one feels a wish to enjoy the fresh air and the songs of the birds in Braidsworth's woods. Oh! Robert, it's a fearful thing, being in such a prison as you—"

" I've had a week of it, lying here, my lass. The doctor tells me every time he comes into the room it will be my prison for the short time I shall have to spend on earth," said the invalid, with calm despair. "Dear mother, go down to father, and leave Sarah and me together for a short time."

"Thou'lt do thyself an injury by talking so," sobbed Mrs. Fisher.

"You shall take cousin's place in a quarter-of-an-hour, at the farthest," said her son. "Go down and see if father wants anything. Poor fellow, he has had no one to attend to his comforts all this weary time."

"Sit down in mother's chair, Sarah," said Robert, in a feeble voice, when the door had closed upon the poor unhappy mother. "It is very sad, is it not, to see poor mother so miserable?"

"It is, indeed, Robert," said his cousin, as she parted the black hair from his damp brow, and put his pillow more comfortably. "How sorry I am you did not send for me earlier."

The poor fellow gave her a look of un-utterable tenderness and love.

"Don't take your hand away, Sarah," said

he, as her hand still lingered about his pillow;
"let me hold it in mine," and Sarah yielded
without hesitation.

Alas! for all his hopes and fears, it lay
quite unmoved in his burning grasp. Had it
trembled in the slightest degree, he might
have hoped, vain and foolish as that hope
must have been; but Robert, with all the
evidence he had, could not delude himself.
From the first, he knew Sarah was devoted
to another.

"Did father tell you I had broken a blood-
vessel, Sarah?" he asked, at last.

"No, Robert, he did not; he never spoke
to me all the way home," Sarah replied.

"I suppose you know it's a very bad sign
to do that," he said, quietly.

"Don't talk in that way, Robert; rather
think about getting better."

"Nothing can ever make me better, lass, I
think. I shall never use paint and canvas
again."

"You will live to be both a good and a

great man yet, cousin Robert, and to see your pictures in many a nobleman's gallery. Come, cheer yourself up, and you will be better in another week or so."

"I might if I could always have you with me, Sarah; I might have a chance then," said Robert, raising himself up in the bed, whilst a flaming red spot mounted to his pale cheek.

"I do not intend leaving you, cousin," was her innocent reply; "but talking in this manner must be very injurious to you. Let us speak of something else."

He dropped her hand—lay down again, and after a pause, said, with quivering lips—

"I think, Sarah, you had better call your aunt, and go to bed yourself, for you must be tired," he said, in his usual tone.

Sarah was not sorry to be released, for her cousin's behaviour perplexed her extremely, and she was becoming very anxious about Fanny, who would be sure to have grown exceedingly impatient by this lengthened waiting. Mr. Fisher had gone to bed, so she would have no trouble in leaving the house, un-observed, by the door leading to the back pre-mises, as Mrs. Fisher, from her son's room, could not hear her departure, and the only thing she had to dread was they might by some means or other discover her absence.

To guard against this, she looked into the invalid's room again to say " good-night " with the bedroom candlestick in her hand, and then stealing noiselessly down-stairs, let her-self out and crept through the farm-yard, like a midnight housebreaker. She felt as if she were committing a guilty action by meet-ing even Fanny without the sanction of her uncle and aunt.

At the gate leading from the farm-yard, she stopped for a minute to gain courage, for she had a dread of meeting one at that hour of the night, whose impetuous character and violent temper had often and often made her tremble, when they lived under the same roof at Braidsworth.

The way in which Fanny left home with a man no one seemed to know anything about, but who Sarah suspected to be a very dangerous and disreputable character, made her flight still worse in Sarah's eyes; and then this meeting by night, with no one near them, had something very alarming to her timid and cowardly imagination, for Sarah was a coward physically, whatever she might be in other respects.

As she still lingered near the gate, which somehow seemed to be the boundary of her safety, simply because she knew her uncle's property ended there, she was more than half tempted to turn back without giving Fanny the coveted interview. There was, however, too much at stake to allow her to indulge this weakness farther, for, instinctively, she felt convinced Fanny possessed information that might materially affect Harry Jobson's fate, and without giving herself time for further reasoning, she ran on as rapidly as she could, until she reached the stile.

"I never did her the slightest harm in all my life," was her thought, as she walked up the field, trembling in every limb at the slightest sound that struck upon her ear. Seeing something dark standing against the doorpost of the barn, she exclaimed—" Fanny, is that you?"

CHAPTER XII.

THE only reply Fanny condescended to make to Sarah's question was to drag her with no gentle action to the place where she had been standing.

"I am very sorry to have kept you waiting such a long time, Fanny," was poor Sarah's timidly uttered excuse, for she could not imagine what would be the other's present mood.

"I did not expect you even as soon as this," said Fanny. "How is your cousin to-night?"

"Robert?" enquired Sarah, in some astonishment at the question.

" Who else do you think I should ask about ?"

" Why, Fanny, I was not aware that you knew of his illness," said the other, in a deprecatory voice.

" I heard that down at the blacksmith's forge, three days ago. I used to loiter up and down before the house when night came on, wishing for the fire, that streamed out upon the road. It made me feel less lonely, from some cause or other, than I did whilst wandering about the fields and lanes."

" Why did you wander about the dark lanes, Fanny ?"

" That I might fall in with you, Sarah, to be sure," replied Fanny. " I was so afraid of being noticed by any one ; and it was not until they told me of Robert Fisher's illness I found out you were not at home. I came upon poor Bobby one night, and walked behind him nearly all the way up to Mr. Fisher's farmstead, without daring to speak to the poor little fellow."

"Where are you living now, Fanny?" asked her companion timidly.

"Sometimes in one place, sometimes in another, lass," said Fanny with a reckless laugh. "We dare not stay for any length of time in one place, I promise you. Bilstone—that's not his right name, Sarah, but it's the one he has adopted for the present—is too much enquired after, to allow him to remain very long in any one locality. He's on the move just at present, or I should have been unable to come here?"

"Would you not leave him, if you could, Fanny?" asked Sarah, in a very melancholy voice.

"Sometimes, I think I would," said the other in an altered tone.

"Why?"

"Because now and then he treats me brutally, and then I vow, in my misery, I will run away and tell all I know—and I know a great many things that would bring him to the gallows—and then when the mood changes with him, and he speaks and looks more kindly, I could almost drown myself for harbouring such treacherous thoughts. Oh ! but it is almost more than human nature can bear when he is in one of his wretched tempers ?"

" I could never love him again, if he once lifted so much as a finger against me, Fanny," said her step-sister, with unusual spirit.

Her companion heaved a deep sigh, but remained for a considerable time in perfect silence, and Sarah did not speak again, she felt so indignant.

Woman's love in many cases, is like the perfume of the camomile, the more it is bruised, the sweeter is the fragrance it exhales; and this unhappy woman's devotion, impure and unhallowed as it was, still burned strong and ardent in a breast that had long ceased to throb with any purer emotion.

Moody and sullen, she was considering the danger she was running in persevering in the new course she was about to undertake.

Her desire was to save Harry Jobson, whom she knew to be perfectly innocent of the crime for which he was about to be tried, as well as the fate to which he would be subjected if found guilty, which he assuredly would be, unless she intervened. But in doing this she jeopardised the safety of Bilstone, alias Smooth, and she could not exactly make up her mind to do that.

The undertaking was a difficult one, but she felt it was to be accomplished, although the risk was very great. The danger, however, so far from deterring her, lent a kind of charm to the affair, for Fanny was by nature, as we have seen, of a bold and daring character, and so long as her guilty associate escaped unpunished, she rather anticipated pleasure or at least excitement in the undertaking with no small degree of impatience.

Her next words, however, did not seem to infer that her thoughts had been dwelling exclusively upon this topic, for she asked, with a

certain amount of tenderness in her tone, unusual with her—

"Did father or mother suffer much at the
last?"

"Father died fearfully, he fretted so much
about poor little Jessie, and uncle said his
heart had been broken before with the bad
times; but our poor mother just went off as
if she had been in a kind of dream."

"Which died first?"

"Mother was the first."

"She always used to say she hoped it would
be so. After their death you came to this
place, I suppose, Sarah?" asked Fanny.

"Uncle Fisher brought me to Chilworth
after the funeral."

"Is he kind, lass? Does he let thee have
thy own way?"

"In some things, Fanny; but not in all,"
was the rejoinder.

"I wish, my dear, I had had less of it—
but all that's over now," said the other in
her usual reckless manner, forming such a

strange contrast to the suppressed feeling she had just exhibited. "But tell me about Harry Jobson. I suppose thou lov'st him still, Sarah ?"

"I do, Fanny," was the poor girl's calm reply.

" And you'd like to clear him of this business ?"

"Oh! Fanny, if you can save him do so," said Sarah, the same feeling animating her breast as that of a despairing mother, yearning to call back the ebbing life of her little one.

"I don't know about that, Sarah; but I will try. If they will take my word— it won't go for much, perhaps—I can save him, but not otherwise."

" Oh! Fanny, dear, what can I say—what can I do in return."

" You often screened me, lass, from your father's anger, when I had been guilty of any trifling fault, and so I owe you a kind turn. Is Harry in good spirits ?"

"Not very, I'm afraid, poor fellow," said Sarah mournfully. "He was very low all the morning before I came away ; oh! Fanny a prison is a frightful place for any one to whom God has given the gifts to enjoy life. I should die if I was shut up there for a week."

"How came they to fix the fire on Harry, pray?" asked Fanny, with sudden interest.

"One of the foundry men promised to lend him something he had been casting from, and poor Harry agreed to meet him at the yard at nine o'clock. He went, and hung about the place as he promised, but the other never came, and some one in passing saw and recognized Harry."

"And was all safe, Sarah, when Harry left the yard?"

"As far as he knew, it was," replied Sarah.

"But the place was all in a blaze by half-past ten, my girl," said Fanny, very abruptly.

"Who told you that, Fanny?" asked Sarah, struck with the observation.

"I can't remember now, lass, for I wasn't

in Braidsworth at the time. Bilstone was away, though, I recollect, and some one came to the village he had left me at, with the news of the fire early the next morning. When are the assizes, lass ?"

" They begin on the third or fourth of November ; and Harry's case, they say, stands first on the list."

" Then on the third of November, Sarah, I will meet you in York."

" But how shall I know where to find you ?"

" You must ask your way to the Druids' Temple," replied Fanny.

" To the where, Fanny ?"

" Thou mustn't forget the name, girl—ask thy way to the Druids' Temple, everybody knows the place," said Fanny.

" When were you at that spot, Fanny ?" demanded her companion, struck with Fanny's minute knowledge of the locality.

" I've been there many and many a time, when I was a bit bairn," said Fanny, in a low tone. "Many a fine summer's day have I strolled about the meadow stringing daisies and buttercups. But all that is over now. That meadow must serve as a place of meeting to us two unhappy beings. It will be almost dark at eight o'clock of a November morning."

"It is very cold standing here, Fanny," said Sarah, shivering as she spoke.

"I'm all in a burning fever, my dear," and Fanny placed her ·hot hand on her companion's icy cheek. "But I must be going now, if I mean to get supper and lodging at the only place I dare apply at hereabout— good-bye, Sarah."

"I would take you with me to uncle Fisher's if—"

"If you dare, Sarah, you would say," cried Fanny, drawing herself up proudly. "I would not put you to so much shame, my lass."

The new risen moon showed her haggard features, as Fanny left the shadow of the old barn. Sarah fancied she could detect a tear coursing down her hollow cheeks, but if it were so, the weakness was only for a moment, for Fanny's hard, impenetrable manner returned, as she held out her hand with the words—

"I will be true to you in this, Sarah, and afterwards we must part for ever."

Sarah's sobs, as she took the proffered hand, prevented her speaking, and with a careless "good night, and mind you remember the Druids' Temple," Fanny drew her shawl around her, and disappeared like a shadow.

After Sarah Crisp's return to Chilworth, her cousin Robert's health began rapidly to improve, but his manner towards her seemed to have changed, all at once, from the greatest cordiality to an appearance of the most utter indifference it is possible to imagine. He no longer cared to have her sitting by his bedside to bear him company as heretofore; if she absented herself for a day, as she occasionally did, when this altered state of things first struck her, Mrs. Fisher was no longer charged with upbraiding messages for her ill-behaviour; her pale but pleasant face—for she had recovered her looks now that she thought Harry Jobson was safe—seemed sadly out of place in that anxious and un-happy sick room, tenanted by Robert and his mother, who really looked ill and unhappy with their cares.

Robert continued to improve so fast, that he was soon able to sit in an arm chair, stuffed so full of hair as to be made as easy and soft as any couch. There he would sit for hours, looking so pale and stern, that Sarah rarely ventured to face him, or, if she did, contrived to make her visits as short as possible. In another week he went into the garden, creep-ing along in his great coat, which hung about his shrivelled limbs like a sack.

It was pleasant to him, in his weak state, to sit in the sun on a bench that faced the south, and watch with a sort of lazy in-terest the autumn treasures that Mrs. Fisher's garden possessed, with a volume of Spenser lying open before him. There he would linger for hours, when the day was warm, sometimes sauntering slowly along with his hands behind him, looking as much like an old man as a young fellow of his age could do; sometimes watching the flight of the pigeons, as they whirled round the farmstead, and feeling, in his weakness, how happy must be an existence such as theirs; anon coming up to the gate, and leaning over to catch the sound of his mother's and Sarah's voices in the kitchen; then stealing away to saunter backward and forward once more at his old pace, and with his old gait. Such was Robert's life for the first two or three weeks after he began to recover his strength.

As soon as he was able to walk so far, he went to the wood, and found the exact spot where Sarah had sat that night on which he had so wildly and madly dreamed she might some day be his wife. There was no shame in poor Robert's heart, as he flung himself on the mossy trunk of the tree, that still looked so fresh and green, and gave himself up to a wild burst of anguish that was all the more intense because it had been so long stifled and smothered in his heart. His grief was so vehement and uncontrollable, that it startled even himself, for he never felt until now, when he knew she could never be his, how very dear Sarah Crisp had become to him; to have her sweet presence ever with him; to hear her gentle voice ever murmuring in his ear, and to feel her soft hands ever ministering to his wants, was a happiness that he could never possess; another had been preferred before him, and Robert schooled his heart to submit to his fate.

He sat up, and his gaze involuntarily rested upon the little lake, the calm beauty of which on that vividly remembered evening had sunk so deep into his heart. He remembered, with scarcely an effort, how the sunset had tinged its water with a golden hue, whilst the shadow of the tree, beneath which they sat, repeated itself in the water below; he remembered, with a kind of mournful pleasure, how the stars had come out one by one in the grey sky until the whole firmament was studded with their glorious lights; he remembered how Sarah had sat and looked, and moved and spoke; how he had helped her over the stiles, her hands trembling as well as his own when they chanced to come in contact, and how they lingered as they reached the top of the hill that overlooked Chilworth to catch one parting glimpse of the beautiful twilight before it faded entirely from their sight, and again his eyes became suffused, and he could scarcely help crying in the utter desolation of his heart.

Robert felt that his cousin could never love him, that she was irrevocably engaged to another, and, come weal or come woe, that other was the only being whom Sarah Crisp could stand at the altar and vow to honour and obey. Certain misery might be her lot, as certain misery would be his; but, at any rate, one grief—the presence of which lay like an incubus upon his heart—would not enter into the portion of her inheritance. She would be loved in return for the pure love she had to give; and this requital of her love would considerably lighten the burden she might be called upon to bear.

The conflict that his soul had to sustain was truly a most terrible one. He had quick, ardent feelings, and from childhood had been remarkable for very violent, but generous passions, which were, it must be confessed, hidden beneath an exceedingly cold and indifferent exterior, that had not only deceived, but were totally misunderstood by those amongst whom he lived, few of whom appreciated the noble, yet tender nature, the seeds of which had been sown, as it would almost seem, by the winds of chance.

Robert threw himself down again on that mossy couch, and lay with his arms tightly pressed across his chest, as if with the vain hope of stilling the wild storm that was raging in his heart, which panted and struggled fearfully. He prayed that it might break—that it might stand still instantaneously—that it might cease to beat—for he was more than half mad with the utter misery that seemed to hem him in on every side. He tried to drive Sarah from his mind, and the more he endeavoured to forget her, so much the more vividly did sweet pale face rise up before him, with the sad, calm smile that seemed habitual to her features. In her plain black dress, with a white muslin handkerchief fastened over her bosom, did she rise up before his mind's eye, and with a deep groan Robert Fisher sprang to his feet, and rushing rather than walking forward, leaned for support against the giant tree whose shadow he had so lately watched in the water beneath.

Why was it, he asked himself, that he was so miserable? For what had so many scalding tears been shed, and so many groans wrung from his nearly bursting heart? What was it that had undermined his strength, brought a raging fever into his blood, and laid him for weeks on a sick bed ? What was it that induced in him these wild and fearful thoughts, that made him shrink and tremble for himself as he looked down with gloomy madness at the deep dark water that lay so still at his very feet ?

It was a woman—a pale, timid, meek-eyed, sweet-faced, tender-hearted girl, without a friend but himself in the world—and this girl he saw daily and hourly ; heard the accents of her voice uttering the homely precepts of daily life, and saw her moving, quiet and serene, about the house that had sheltered him from childhood. Was it not madness to erect such a being into a goddess, endow her with attributes such as no woman out of Eden ever possessed, and to vow that utter misery and desolation should henceforth be his portion, solely because she could never be his ! Was it manly ? Was it wise ? Was it not the height of folly to act in this way ?

His lips moved, though it is doubtful if a

prayer passed through them for strength to struggle through this, his hour of trial, for his heart was too proud to implore even the help of God in his sore trouble and affliction. Presently a strange calm stole over him, and his mind became purified and strengthened by the terrible conflict it had sustained, reminding one of how the firmament clears after a storm. He glanced up at the sky, and smiled even, as he observed how fair and sunny it looked, and a thanksgiving burst from his lips, as he felt conscious he had gained a terrible yet noble victory over himself.

Whilst still standing in the shadow of the tree Robert saw a dark figure tripping down the walk that led through the fields from Chilworth homestead to the wood, and a second look told him it was Sarah Crisp.

Curious to see what she would do, Robert clambered up the bank as quickly as his strength would allow him, and concealed himself amongst the bushes that grew in wild luxuriance about the spot, whilst Sarah, quite unconscious that she was watched, came on towards the mossy seat, her pace becoming slower the nearer she approached. She lingered in passing the pool, and threw in a pebble, watching the bubbles as they rose, and then, darting a quick, inquisitive glance round, came up to the seat, and sitting down, she drew a letter from her pocket and began to read.

END OF VOL. II.

T. C. NEWBY, 30, Welbeck Street, Cavendish Square, London.

MAY, 1872.

MR. NEWBY'S NEW PUBLICATIONS.

NEW NOVELS.

In Three Vols.   Price 31s. 6d.

THE GLADSTONES.

By FRANK TROLLOPE,

Author of "The Marked Man," "An Old Man's Secret," "A Right Minded Woman," &c.

In Three Vols.   Price 31s. 6d.

SECOND EDITION.

FIRM IN THE STRUGGLE.

By EMMA PICKERING,

Author of "Forsaking all Others," &c.

"Miss Pickering always writes like a lady of education and refinement. The dialogue of 'Firm in the Struggle' is clever, abounding in smartness and piquancy. Amongst trees, and flowers, and quiet country scenes, she is thoroughly at home, and these she sketches with happy effect and truthfulness "—ALBION.

"The contemptuous scorn of the usually gentle Avice, the thorough goodness of Hugh, or the affectation of Maud are drawn most naturally, while Lily and Bessie are perfect characters." - JOHN BULL.

"The story is extremely interesting, and never flags for a single page. We scarcely know a fiction of modern times in which the characters are so well sketched and sustained. Many of the descriptions of country life and scenery are quite equal to those so admirably depicted in 'Adam Bede.'"—DAILY GUARDIAN.

"Miss Pickering's truthful pictures of country life and scenery are not surpassed by any of the female novelists of the present time."—BRIGHTON GUARDIAN.

"This novel is fair and fresh as May flowers, and deserves for its ability of treatment and purity of tone the highest praise. All the characters are well and evenly drawn, and show a great harmony of treatment. It is a story of life: full of life's sorrows, temptations, joys, and triumphs."—DRAWING-ROOM GAZETTE.

"The skill of the authoress has allowed her to rise into the higher regions of imaginative lore."—BELL'S MESSENGER.

In 3 Vols. (In JUNE.)

WILD WOOD.

In 3 Vols.

CLUMBER CHASE.

By GEORGE GORDON SCOTT.

"A thoroughly fresh, sparkling and singularly original work, but what is far more wonderful—the source considered—a pure and healthy one. The dialogue throughout is racy and brilliant. Altogether the reading of *Clumber Chase*, after the stifling moral—or rather immoral—atmosphere of the general run of modern novels, has been to us like a blow on the Moors, amid the fresh purple heather."—BELL'S MESSENGER.

"The most clever, brilliant, and witty novel that has appeared for years."—DAILY GUARDIAN.

"It will unquestionably afford much amusement, and create no little interest."—MORNING POST.

In 3 Vols.

ROBERT BLAKE OF RINGWOOD.

From the *Times*.

"It commands the respect due to a pure and wholesome tone of thought, and seeks to interest us by legitimate delineation of character, rather than to thrill us by the startling turn of an ingenious plot. It neither demoralizes our moral nor bewilders our mental faculties."

MISCELLANEOUS WORKS.

In 1 Vol., post 8vo., 12s.

MEXICO UNDER MAXIMILIAN.

By J. J. KENDALL,

Late Captain H.M. 44th and 6th Regiments, and subsequently in the service of his late Majesty

THE EMPEROR OF MEXICO.

"The author has taken great pains to obtain authentic information, and as to the interest of the book there can be no doubt."—*Morning Post.*

"The author is a close observer of men and manners, and is every inch a traveller and a soldier. His book is most interesting."—*Inverness Advertiser.*

"Much useful and interesting information is contained in this volume. Its perusal cannot be attended with other than a feeling of pleasure."—*Court Circular.*

"'Mexico under Maximilian' (Newby), by J. J. Kendall, late Captain H.M. 44th and 6th Regiments, and subsequently in the service of his late Majesty the Emperor of Mexico, is an interesting chapter of the history of Mexico under the unfortunate Emperor Maximilian, related by an eye-witness, and one who personally shared in the many dangers and horrors of the time. Captain Kendall writes graphically, and the story he tells loses none of its thrilling interest in his manner of telling it. The incidents are all of them attractive, and are described naturally and with no attempt at exaggeration."

"A very readable and amusing book. Captain Kendall gives us interesting sketches of the natural capabilities of the country, and the social habits of the people."—*John Bull.*

In 1 Vol., 7s. 6d.

ON SEX IN THE WORLD TO COME,

AN ESSAY.

BY THE REV. G. D. HOUGHTON, B.A.

————— " What if Earth
Be but the shadow of Heaven, and things therein
Each to other like, more than on Earth is thought."

"This is the work of a profound scholar, and is deserving much attention."—*New Quarterly Review.*

In 2 Vols.   Price 10s.

SHELLEY AND HIS WRITINGS,

By C. S. MIDDLETON, Esq.

"Never was there a more perfect specimen of biography." — WALTER SAVAGE LANDOR, ESQ.

"Mr. Middleton has done good service. He has carefully sifted the sources of information we have mentioned, has made some slight addition, and arranged his materials in proper order and in graceful language. It is the first time the mass of scattered information has been collected, and the ground is therefore cleared for a new generation of readers."—ATHENÆUM.

"The life of the poet which has just appeared, and which was much required, is written with much beauty of expression and clearness of purpose. Mr. Middleton's book is a masterly performance."— SOMERSET GAZETTE.

"Mr. Middleton has displayed great ability in following the poet through all the mazes of his life and thoughts. We recommend the work as lively, animated, and interesting. It contains many curious disclosures."— SUNDAY TIMES.

In 1 Vol., Post 8vo.   Price 10s. 6d.

HEROIC   IDYLS,

AND OTHER POEMS,

By WALTER SAVAGE LANDOR.

"These Idyls may take their place with those heretofore given us by Mr. Landor. Judged of simply by their merits, they compel that rare admiration which we yield only to noble ideals made palpable by true heart. As recent works they claim the tribute of our wonder, no less than of our delight."—*Athenæum.*

"The same classical feeling which has given a harmony even to the most fanciful of his 'Imaginary Conversations,' and moulded the thoughts of an English poet in the lines of Greek simplicity and beauty, is to be found here, as delicately marked as ever. Few artistes of modern times have taken a larger range, or have carried out a clearly conceived purpose with a steadier hand. When Mr. Landor is gone, we shall have lost at once the founder, and almost the only follower of a peculiar and grand school."—*Saturday Review.*

In 1 Vol., post 8vo., price 5s.

SPIRITUALISM AND THE AGE WE LIVE IN,

By MRS. CROWE,

Author of "Night Side of Nature," "Ghost Stories," &c.

THE FOURTH EDITION, ILLUSTRATED.

In 1 Vol., post 8vo., price 7s. 6d.

A NARRATIVE OF ADVENTURES IN FRANCE AND FLANDERS,

DURING THE LATE WAR,

By CAPTAIN EDWARD BOYS, Royal Navy.

" Readers will like this curious narrative, which has all the charm of truthfulness, which few writers, excepting De Foe, could have written half so truthfully ; and Captain Boys' interesting and patriotic story is all truth in itself."—ILLUSTRATED TIMES.

"Many of the events recorded have long since become matters of history ; they are, however, so mixed up with personal adventures, simple truth conveyed in a simple form, that we read on with unflagging attention."—MORNING ADVERTISER.

"Every youth in Her Majesty's dominions should read these adventures."—DAILY POST.

www.ingramcontent.com/pod-product-compliance
Lightning Source LLC
Chambersburg PA
CBHW021047030726
47496CB00006B/1723